Not long ago, in the unexplored reaches of an un-
mapped swamp, the creative genius of one man collided
with another's evil plan, and a monster was born.

Too powerful to be destroyed, too intelligent to be captured, this immensely powerful being still pursues its savage dream . . . .

A Melniker-Uslan Production of a
Wes Craven Film
Louis Jourdan   Adrienne Barbeau
Based upon characters appearing in magazines
published by DC Comics, Inc.
Produced by Benjamin Melniker and
Michael E. Uslan
Written and Directed by Wes Craven
An Avco Embassy Pictures Release

SCIENCE TRANSFORMED HIM INTO A MONSTER.
LOVE CHANGED HIM EVEN MORE!

TM & © DC Comics, Inc. 1981

A NOVEL BY
DAVID HOUSTON AND LEN WEIN

TOR

A TOM DOHERTY ASSOCIATES BOOK
Distributed by Pinnacle Books, New York

This is a work of fiction. All the characters and events portrayed in this book are fictional, and any resemblance to real people or incidents is purely coincidental.

SWAMP THING

A Tor Book

Published by Tom Doherty Associates, 8-10 W. 36th St., New York City, N.Y. 10018
First printing, April 1982
ISBN: 0-523-48039-3

Distributed by Pinnacle Books, 1430 Broadway, New York, N.Y. 10018

1

Things of the swamp know each other.

Mottled bullfrogs make way for lumbering alligators; the rare snarl of a wildcat sends creatures under cover; water moccasins must move invisibly in order to deceive; when a deer runs, the air fills with herons and flamingos.

And every living thing understands the wind.

But the noisy helicopter that slapped the air violently on a recent summer afternoon could not be taken for granted. The perpetual symphony of nature quieted; the creatures shrank back and listened.

A possum looked up from the torn catfish on which it dined. It never saw the loud machine menacing it from the sky, but nevertheless it bolted for the fragile cover of a palm bog. The murky water of a vast shallow lake vibrated, broke out in chills under the reverberant air. Fish dove, as during a storm, though the clear air was hot. Birds cowered in the cypress trees, unsure whether to fly or hide.

The copter came down low over the water and skimmed toward a misty mound of green at the tip of a peninsula that looked like the finger of a giant mossy hand. The hand was one of countless limbs stretching out from more solid bodies of land into the aimless currents of the waters which were thick and brown with a conspiracy of life and decay.

There were no signposts. From the air, direction-finding could be a matter of luck.

"The damn place is invisible," muttered the copter pilot, a young man with short red hair; he was dressed in jeans and a Western shirt. He and his two passengers craned forward to see the land at the distant edge of the water rushing below them.

"Supposed to be invisible," said the man next to him. This was Charlie Tanner, a weather-worn gray-haired man who clutched a map and glanced at it nervously. "I've made this trip before, but nothing out there looks familiar. You'd think the trees and islands wander around and rearrange themselves just to be confusing. We could be over any number of inundated lowlands; they all look alike."

"All I'm doing is following a compass," said the pilot. "You sure as hell better know where we're supposed to set down."

"I think it's that land jutting out dead ahead."

"What're you going to do when I let you off? Swim?"

"That's been worked out."

The third occupant of the copter leaned forward between the two men. "Where's the nearest good restaurant?" asked Alice Cable.

"About sixty miles back the way we came," the pilot said with a chuckle.

"Depends," Charlie interjected. "If you're human, the best restaurants are all the way back in Washington. If you're an alligator, it's wherever we land."

Cable nodded and smiled. "I brought the wrong clothes," she said. She was pretty, in her late twenties, dressed for work in office or laboratory: in a tailored gray-blue suit.

"That's it," Charlie said, pointing ahead.

"Oh," said the pilot, "that's a boat. I thought it was a floating log. Okay, down we go." He adjusted his controls; the copter banked as it slowed and descended.

Charlie turned to Cable. "Thank your lucky stars you're coming in at the end of this venture. You might have been stuck down there for months, years."

Below, under cover of trees and tall ferns on almost dry land, sentient eyes watched the copter descend. The eyes belonged to a man named Ferret and the several men who looked to him for truth. The men were hiding; they kept their weapons low to the ground but dry. Ferret alone was on his feet, trusting that as long as he did not move no person or thing would notice him. While his reasoning was sound, anyone who did see him would find him difficult to forget. His features were gaunt and geometrical, as if carved out of slate; his eyes were hard as broken glass. The loose-fitting clothes he wore were army surplus, utilitarian jungle camouflage; and from his belt dangled a pearl-handled .45 and a polished machete. The gold earring he wore labeled him a pirate—which is why he delighted in wearing it.

The helicopter, its pontoons approaching the water, dipped out of sight; and Ferris gestured for his men to follow him. They got silently to their feet.

"Will he go to the chopper?" one of the men asked his leader.

Ferret shook his head.

He led his men through ferns and across a mossy clearing—away from the landing helicopter—toward the water on the other side of the peninsula.

"Are you sure they don't know we're here?" another man whispered hoarsely.

Ferret nodded.

The copter descended onto a sheltered lagoon covered with water lilies, which pitched and tossed with the powerful downdraft of the rotors. There the pontoons touched down, and the copter was at rest.

Cable pointed to the woods where Ferret and his men moved among the giant ferns. "What's that?" she asked.

"Deer, perhaps," said Charlie.

A blue outboard was approaching from across the field of water lilies. Two men were in it. The one who steered had a semiautomatic weapon slung over one shoulder; it looked out of place with his nonmilitary, Joe College attire. The other man, similarly casually dressed, fumbled with a suitcase and duffle bag as the boat pulled alongside the copter.

Charlie helped Cable step onto the pontoon. "Holland insisted on locating out here," he said. "Not just for the practical reason of privacy and security, but because of

7

some romantic notion of his that the swamp is where life is. He loves it out here." A mosquito dug into Charlie's neck and he slapped it to a dark red spot. "He's certainly right about this being where life is. There are probably more living things per square inch here than anywhere else."

The man with the luggage tossed his things to the pilot, who stowed them in the rear seat.

"In fact," Charlie continued, "one of the larger life forms out here nailed the technician you're replacing."

The departing passenger heard this and said, "A woman? They sent a woman out here?"

"What the hell does she look like?" asked Charlie. "A penguin?" He laughed to ward off the meaning behind the man's words. He had no wish to alarm the newcomer.

As they stepped into the boat, the new copter passenger laughed, too, a different sort of laugh that Cable did not find reassuring. The weapon worn by the boatman did not reassure her either.

The boatman said, "Hi, Charlie. Good trip back to civilization?"

"Quite pleasant, Bill," he said. "Why are we losing that one?" He gestured toward the man entering the copter.

The rotors revved again, and whined and flapped.

"He couldn't take it any more," said Bill with a shrug. "But I guess he's been here longer than most. You know, the scientists have it pretty easy, compared with the rest of us. They get to stay inside. We live with the mosquitos and water moccasins . . . and just this constant smell of decay. It's not strong, but it adds up after a few months." Having stacked Cable's luggage in the boat and cast off the loose line that held them at the pontoon, the boatman turned to Cable with a self-approved smile and waited to be introduced.

"This is Cable," Charlie informed him. "She's our new electronics man, uh, person. Computers and instrumentation. She'll work directly with the Hollands. Cable, meet Bill Darkow, one of our more loyal guardians."

8

Cable wanted to ask why guardians were necessary, but her chance was obliterated by the almost simultaneous roars of the rising copter and the departing boat. Lily pads flew through the air; one slapped the side of her face.

"How far—?" Cable shouted over the noise.

"You can see our pier now," Charlie said; now that the copter had risen, he spoke in a normal voice. "Too much overhang to allow the copter to get very close. Short boat trip. See the lab—that gray steeple through the trees?"

"Looks like a church."

"It was."

"Out here in the middle of nowhere?"

"There's a good stretch of dry land in there, and what's left of a community. The church was a mission built nearly a hundred years ago. Abandoned, like the town." Charlie ran a hand through his gray hair, which was dampening from the boat's spray, and asked the boatman, "How's your brother? He still with us?"

"Something's bugging him," said Bill, "and I'm damned if I can figure out what."

Bill's twin brother, Sam, was at that moment approaching the opposite side of the peninsula in a blue boat exactly like that in which Cable and Charlie were being ferried.

Sam cut the motor of his boat and listened. The copter was gone, and he could hear, very faintly, the motor of Bill's boat across the finger of land. He heard crying birds and buzzing insects—and sounds that seemed to imply that large creatures were rustling through the underbrush, perhaps creatures as large as men.

His coasting boat carried him under a drapery of Spanish moss; the hull thumped against a cypress root.

He, like his brother, carried a semiautomatic strapped over his shoulder; he slipped it into a more useful position.

The boat continued to drift toward land; he continued to hear the rustling sound. A bullfrog large as a cat plopped into the water as his boat passed the stump on which it sunned.

The rustling sound stopped; so did the sound of Bill's

distant boat. Sam thought he heard a voice, but it could have been so many things.

He stepped shakily out of the boat and, picking his way among cypress roots, made his way to land. The gnarled wood—like twisted bones—was slippery with moss.

Sounds had disturbed him before; now it was silence that made his heart race. Why had the creatures stopped singing? They did that, he knew, when conditions were puzzling to them—as they had when the helicopter approached—and sometimes there were pauses in the chatter of the swamp for no apparent reason. And sometimes the creatures stopped to listen when there were humans nearby. But he knew of no humans with cause to be in the vicinity.

Sam walked slowly, his feet silent on the soft earth, along a path that had been cleared a month ago; already it was being reclaimed by the vegetation of the swamp. Off to the sides, he recalled from earlier trips, were bogs of quicksand invisible under layers of fallen leaves and branches.

He approached a clearing where one of the Project's remote sensors was positioned. The sensors both monitored the conditions of the area and served as a perimeter security system. The sensor up ahead—he could see it, now, in the center of the clearing—was number three; and for no apparent reason, it was dead. Sam wondered why.

He stopped and drew in a sharp breath. Something moved in the clearing. Three men. Had they seen him? Sam doubted it. He held his rifle ready and slipped a walkie-talkie from his belt.

The three men had their backs to him; they looked like mercenary soldiers—in camouflage, high boots, and armed with rifles.

"I'll take the walkie-talkie," said a casual voice behind him. "And the rifle."

Sam turned slowly and looked into the face of a stranger—in a part of the world where there were supposed to be no strangers. This man was a gray skeleton, a tall man with a gold earring. Government dispatches had described such a man, called him extremely dangerous, said his where-abouts were unknown, gave the names by which he was known. Among them was Ferret. The name fell from Sam Darkow's lips.

One of the men—now there were nine of them—approached and asked Ferret, "Take care of him?" He was large, evidently a body-building hobbyist, whose shirt-sleeves were tight as a paint job. His face was oddly boyish, innocent—in fact, stupid.

"Perhaps, Bruno," said Ferret as he tossed the man Sam's radio and weapon, and the pistol he had leveled at Sam's heart.

Sam thought fast, as he had been taught to do, and spun around to charge back toward his boat—while the brutish Bruno had his hands full and Ferret was unarmed.

Sam made it out of the clearing, but then Ferret's men forced him off the trail, toward the quicksand bogs.

Ferret himself was in the lead. It seemed to be understood among the men that their leader would be the one to bag the quarry, and the others were just helping him out a little.

Sam's left boot slid into quicksand; he pulled it out with a sickening plopping sound. That slowed him down enough. The men blocked every turn. Ferret, with a glee-ful whoop, tackled the young man and sat on his legs. Sam looked up into the barrels of an assortment of pistols and rifles.

Two of the men hauled Sam to his feet.

"What do you want?" Sam asked.

The tall skeleton shrugged cheerfully. "Anonymity, among other things. I doubt if there's much you can do for me." Ferret slipped a glove onto his right hand and thrust it into the deep cargo pocket of his fatigues. Something in there was moving. He pulled out a large cottonmouth, holding it behind its head; the poisonous fangs were already bared in a wide-open mouth.

"No," said Sam, the color draining from his face, "that's ridiculous. You can't—"

Ferret touched the head of the cottonmouth to Sam's

bare forearm. The fangs sank in, and Sam screamed.

A great heron was startled and flapped into the sky.

As Cable and Charlie stepped onto the pier, they heard what sounded like a human cry. It echoed. Bill Darkow heard it too. They listened, but there was no second cry, and the birds and insects seemed undisturbed.

"Weird, huh?" said Charlie. "Local fishermen think this place is haunted."

Cable's eyes rested on a row of gravestones, each angled slightly differently due to the subsidence of the ground. Evidently the graveyard had belonged to the church.

"I don't know where we are, Toto," Cable muttered to herself with a brave smile, "but it sure isn't Kansas."

"What?" Charlie asked.

"Nothing," said Cable.

2

Alice Cable was a practical scholar in search of . . . something. Something that would ever after focus her energies, her intelligence, her drive, her love of her work. She had a phobia of jobs that, in the last analysis, were nothing but production lines — even research and development positions often meant nothing more than tinkering together one patentable gadget after another for an electronics firm.

At graduation time—she had been near the top of her class at MIT—she had been one of those courted arduously by the personnel departments of worldwide video, communications, and computer concerns. She had flown with others of her classmates to visit the firms, at company expense, to examine job possibilities. Enviably, it had been the applicants who interviewed the companies and grandly turned them down. But her group had dwindled as the others had accepted well-paying positions in industry.

She had looked at them with the thought: How can you settle for so little challenge merely for the money and the fringe benefits? She had also envied them their satisfaction.

She had gone back to school and obtained a master's degree. With it, she had become a troubleshooter for the Government's diverse installations. But that wasn't *it*, either. She wanted something more vital. Had they been enlisting colonists for Mars, she would have signed up without a second thought.

Men, as a race, did not seem to understand Alice Cable. Though she was pretty—slender, with brown hair and

13

regular features—she was too intense. Though she was not "tough," she seldom laughed or smiled, and this made her seem remote. "You're a better man than they are," a college counselor had told her once. "That doesn't make any sense," Cable replied, truly perplexed.

No one had called her Alice since high school. She was just Cable.

Her attempts at love had led her into promiscuity for a brief period during college—until she met Les Brand, who made her forget and regret the others. Brand was a painter, a maverick out of the mainstream of art who was, if anything, more intense and hard-working than she. They had met by accident on campus the day he dropped out and went back to his art; it had been cold and windy, and she had helped him gather up his blowing sketches. Their love had also been cold and windy, and the values they shared had kept blowing away. His spirit of doom had dragged her down; her spirit of adventure had made him anxious. Her love of the real world had clashed with the romantic fantasy he tried to bring into existence, a romantic fantasy in which he felt safe because it was not real.

She had no notion where Les Brand was today, or what he might be doing. He was her last love, several years ago.

Her call to Holland's lab in the no-man's land of a Southern swamp was no quirk of fate. She had known of the existence of the lab—which had been kept out of popular science journals—due to the government's participation in the funding of whatever Holland was doing. But not even government files revealed the nature of his work. That, she had deduced from a study of his past achievements.

Three years ago, Holland had reconstructed the primal atmosphere of earth and in it, using Frankenstein-like surges of lightning, he had caused carbon, hydrogen, nitrogen, oxygen, sulphur and phosphorus to form a living compound. Holland had built an amino acid to order, and he had watched one of his primal cells (some called them "artificial cells") divide.

14

When last heard from and written about, Holland was proposing to develop microscopic organisms that would devour disease-causing microbes. "Is *this* how we'll cure the common cold?" asked one journal in headlines. "Could this mean the end of humanity?" asked another. A last item on the subject indicated that Holland had shelved such experiments "until such time as genetic engineering provides more answers than it does questions."

The hidden lab, Cable reasoned, had to be carrying on Holland's controversial research with recombinant DNA—away from the prying eyes of the press. The government involvement in funding suggested there might be military implications in his work. His need for an electronics expert suggested an endeavor that was highly complex, indeed.

Her predecessor had been eaten by an alligator? The notion was so absurd, and suggested such carelessness, that the fact also struck her as funny.

As she stepped onto dry land, she suddenly wondered: What had the electronics man been doing out in the swamp? She had thought the scientific team would stay close to the lab.

But she did not ask the question because "dry land" turned out to be mud, and she sank in it to her ankles.

Several armed men approached from the underbrush.

"Where's Sam?" Bill Darkow asked them.

"Said he wanted to check on something," said one of the men. "One of the sensors, probably. Welcome back, sir." The man turned his attention to Charlie. "I see you brought us a pretty lady."

"That I did," said the Project administrator.

The men smiled at Cable but seemed more interested in Charlie.

"What did they say in Washington?" another asked.

Charlie offered Cable his arm, to help her pull herself out of the glue-like mud. "That's confidential, Teddy. But, well, you can almost start packing your toothbrush."

"All right!" Teddy said exuberantly. "Then why send us another electronics man . . . woman?"

Cable answered this herself. "Instrumentation and

15

computation are never more vital than when a project is being wrapped up. Whatever we don't do now may never get done.''

"The boss doesn't know, does he?'' another of the men asked. "This morning he was acting like we'll all be here till hell freezes over.''

"I don't suppose he does know,'' said Charlie. "And don't you say anything to him; it's my job—and too complicated to talk about by phone or radio. That's why I didn't call ahead. Hell, I might as well tell you. Government funds are being withdrawn, but some of the private endowments will continue. Holland can go on for a while longer, if he wants to, with a reduced staff.''

Cable looked with dismay at her expensive muddy boots. *They should have told me we'd be roughing it*, she muttered internally; *but then again, I should have guessed it*.

It was easy to see—now that she knew to look—what land was dry path and what around her might be less than solid.

Off to her side of the path were more rows of tilted, eroded gravestones. Parts of a vine-wrapped fence showed how the graveyard had once been made private. Decades ago, she suspected, the water table was lower here, and the land was drier. Something about the unkempt tumble-down graveyard gave her a chill. The graveyard itself was dead.

So was the church; but now a bright electric parasite dwelled within it. In the late afternoon light, which was dimming through the thick live oak and cypress overhead as the sun neared the horizon, the front windows of the old church cast beams of brilliance into the gloomy swamp. Pieces of stained glass still clung to the leading.

Of weather-warped frame, the old church had a listing steeple and a bell that was rusted tight to its axle. Missing boards, like wounds, suggested that new interior walls had been erected and that the lab was mainly taking advantage of the stone foundation. There were gaping holes in the roof through which trusses could be seen—telling Cable in advance that the lab would be a large and high enclosure unobstructed by columns or supporting walls.

There was a rock chimney, and a wisp of smoke rose from it—residue from some experiment, Cable guessed, as there was no need for heat in the sultry swamp.

There were several dilapidated frame shacks—complete with verandas and porch swings—near the church. Charlie led her toward one of them.

"Why the cutback?" Cable asked him. "Just budget cuts, or is Washington paranoid about having a hand in what's going on here?"

Charlie shot her a diplomat's benign smile and said only, "This cabin is your place, and it's also the electronics command center."

The porch planks gave and the screen door screeched, but inside Cable found herself in clean, comfortable quarters—two good-sized rooms and a kitchen and bathroom. Four bunks in the bedroom indicated that a concession had been made to her womanhood; the three men who might be sharing had been placed elsewhere. The living room was really a workroom, her own lab.

There a row of workbenches held state-of-the-art analyzers and computation equipment. Cable pointed offhandedly for her baggage to be put in the bedroom and stepped directly to the instruments.

"You probably haven't seen half of this stuff," Charlie said. "It's all new. This—" he laid his hand on a knob-encrusted green-metal box "—just arrived when I was leaving to pick you up in Washington. It's a—"

Cable nodded. "It's a laser-induced subsonic field generator." Her smile told Charlie that she was showing off a little and enjoying it. "It gives double readings in the 3200 band, right? I've got a trick for fixing that."

Charlie stared at her, surprised, and then laughed. "Just our luck," he said. "They send someone who knows what she's doing the very week they start pulling us out."

"I may stay awhile," Cable said casually. "If I'm needed."

"You can't tell me all this appeals to you!"

17

"I brought my bug spray." She added, more seriously, "Besides, I've got to know what kind of project can use such a fantastic array of equipment. What's he working on —specifically?"

"Who?"

"Holland. You must know more than you've told me so far."

Charlie leaned against the back of a metal folding chair. "He's doing something so hush-hush no one even asks. It has something to do with plants."

"What?"

Charlie squirmed uneasily; he did not know how much he was at liberty to say. Before he could deliver a guarded answer, there was an insistent buzz.

"Intercom," Charlie explained. He lifted a conventional wall telephone mounted by the kitchen door and said, "Hi, boss. We're getting settled."

While Charlie reported on pleasant flights, good weather, an effective landing and an organized reception committee, Cable moved closer to the equipment. She stumbled over a pair of boots and two stuffed duffle bags that had been tossed under the bench. She looked at Charlie inquiringly.

He covered the mouthpiece with his hand and told her: "Bill and Sam, the twins, stayed here till recently. Apparently one of them hasn't finished moving out."

As Charlie returned to his conversation, Cable began switching on pieces of equipment. A small CRT monitor lighted up with a message. In simplified computer type, it said: "SENSOR OUT/SECTION THREE."

She found a clipboard on the bench that listed twelve sectors, with twelve sensors that recorded sound, wind velocity, light level, and air mixture with emphasis on toxic gasses, temperature and humidity. Number three seemed to be out—unless the display was being misled by an internal problem.

Cable made a mental connection but thought very little of it: *They said Bill's brother went out to check on something; maybe it was the sensor.*

18

Charlie said, "Sure, Alec, right away," and dropped the phone back onto its cradle. "C'mon," he said to Cable, taking her arm, "the emperor wants to meet you."

"Charlie," she started to say, "there's a sensor—"

"You can get to work a little later," he said impatiently. "Incidentally—" he flipped a switch at the door "—this is a master that cuts off most of what's running in here. Saves your having to hit 'em one at a time."

"But computer core—"

"Depends on where things are plugged in. This doesn't turn off your refrigerator either."

Between the cabin and the church—no more than sixty feet—ran a reed-lined stream over which there was a rickety wooden bridge. The stream widened into an inlet leading to the east side of the peninsula. A man Cable had not met stood on the bridge and yelled instructions to several men in a blue boat approaching from the inlet. "Get that thing out of sight! You want it picked up on a spy satellite? No boats in sight; you know that."

The boat nosed in to the shallow bank; the men jumped out and hauled it toward a shelter of camouflage net that was stretched among trees to the side of the church.

Cable frowned. This looked more and more like a military installation—something she had not been led to expect.

The man on the bridge—in his fifties, dark-haired, wearing khaki trousers and shirt—sized up Cable as she came near. She did not like the way he looked at her; he was not taking her seriously. When he smiled, it was insolent, assuming, insulting by virtue of being flattering.

He spoke to Charlie first. "Charlie. Welcome back."

"Harry," Charlie said with a polite nod.

"This the new electronics officer?"

Charlie nodded. "Cable, this is Colonel Harry Ritter, project field supervisor."

Cable and Ritter shook hands. She said, "Why so cautious?"

"Because it's necessary," Ritter said evenly.

"Why?" she persisted.

19

"Standard operating procedure," he said.

"Standard, for what?"

"For operations such as this."

Ritter and Charlie walked briskly toward the church; Cable hung back, puzzled, watching the men camouflage the harmless blue boat; then she ran to catch up with Charlie and Ritter. She slapped a mosquito that was drinking from her forearm.

The two men were not speaking. Cable said, "I want to run a check on all the sensors right away. At least one is reading malfunction."

Ritter said peremptorily, "That's no surprise. They rot in a week in these damn swamps." To Charlie he said, "Did they change their minds?"

"They?"

"The sub-sub-committe on whatever we are."

"No. They feel that Holland's done pretty much what he came down here to do. As much as is practical, anyway. Now they want him, his substance and all the materials, back in Washington where they can keep them safe."

Ritter slowed his steps. "You mean, don't you Charlie, that the money's run out, and they want the stuff not to keep it safe but to lock it away for good? Or kill it?"

Charlie said uneasily, "I don't think that's exactly what I mean, but I suppose it's close."

They stopped at the big double doors to the church.

Ritter said, quietly, "Charlie. Out with it. Is there anything wrong that you know of? Why *now,* why so suddenly?"

Charlie bit his lip. "A rumor," he said with a shrug. "Somebody told somebody that Arcane's got wind of the project."

Cable's ears bristled. Arcane. She knew the name; he was wanted for every brand of industrial espionage known to the legal profession. "But I thought Arcane was dead," she said.

"He is," said Ritter.

"His body was never found," Charlie reminded them, "and they say his financial resources—if he's still alive—

20

are virtually limitless."

"Who said that?" Ritter asked sharply. "Who said that Arcane was onto this?"

Charlie fumbled for words and finally said, "Well, nobody's exactly taking credit for it. You know Washington."

Ritter rested his hand on the big, brass doorhandle. "I know something else: what Holland thinks of Arcane. Alec lost half-a-dozen patents to the man, if he's alive. Remember that biodegradable solvent Arcane marketed for millions? All it takes is for one idiot to spill this to Holland and he'll shut up shop like a clam . . . and *everybody's* profits will go to hell in a handbasket. Do you agree?" Ritter's narrow dark eyes bored a hole in Charlie's.

"Yes," said Charlie.

Ritter said to Cable, "That goes for you, too. Don't tell him."

She said, "I understand your concern."

Ritter clearly wanted a more positive response from her, but he accepted what he got. He swung open the church doors.

3

With a squawk of rusted hinges, Cable, Charlie and Ritter passed inside. The doors were shut behind them by an armed man standing guard.

Cable faced an unadorned modern wall that was criss-crossed with pipe and conduit and wires. As she had suspected, a laboratory had been built within the shell of the old church—which would look like nothing more than an old church to the spy satellites Ritter seemed paranoid about.

Between her and the wall stood the guard's desk, on which a radio played popular music, and a quiet but conspicuous electric generator the size of a small truck.

Of the red and green lights over the door, the green was lighted. It reminded Cable of television studios she had visited.

Ritter pointed out a glowing box by the door. He said, "I keep the number of people near him to a minimum. Your prints were programmed in this morning. Try it out."

Cable thought: If so few can get in, I wonder if Holland goes out much. Does he know that there's a small army guarding him out here?

She inserted her hand in the slot of frosted glass.

With a thunk of servo-motors, the door glided open.

Cable had not known what to expect; what she saw took her breath away. It was a bio/botanical laboratory, obviously, and much more. Gleaming, light-pulsing instruments were arrayed within towering tangles of glass and stainless-steel tubing. Rack upon rack of flasks contained rainbows of earth-colored fluids, and dark tanks bubbled vigorously.

Ladders were positioned at two-story-high shelves that contained bottles of chemicals, and other shelves holding a library's supply of books. Taller ladders led to an upper balconied level that evidently housed living quarters.

Where a choir once sang, there now was an arboretum encased by jewel-like facets of glass and flooded with beams of blue light. The tall trees and flowering plants it contained were so perfect they seemed artificial; they stretched upward toward the sun.

The ceiling of the lab was a grid of glass panes that admitted sunlight through what was left of the old church roof. Through the integument, Cable saw the eroded planks and beams of the old church structure, which were moss-covered and draped with flowering vines. The oblique rays of the setting sun made the blossoms incandescent; the artificial suns over the arboretum were blue by comparison.

Charlie said something to her.

"What?" she said, distracted.

"I said, 'Gotta hand it to Ritter.' He certainly gave Holland everything he asked for."

"Ritter built this?" Cable asked incredulously. "I thought he was just in charge of security."

"That is more or less all he does now. He was more active in the beginning. Even had something to do with funding."

"I did my job," Ritter said, returning from the door, where he had been double-checking the seal. He caught Charlie by the elbow and ushered him away from Cable, toward a private corner. "Charlie, I want to hear every detail of this Arcane business, now," he said forcefully.

Cable began to follow them. "About that sensor out in sector three—"

Charlie stopped. "Uh, yes," he said—annoyed not so much at Cable as at the fact that there was a problem—"you go out there and take a look." He broke off with a shrug and hurried after Ritter.

Cable muttered aloud, but to herself, "Me? Go out in

the swamp? Who with?" She turned and walked toward the arboretum. After a moment, she heard voices from inside.

"Any luck?" said a man.

"Try wiggling your fingers," said a woman.

Cable saw the two before she passed through the open portal in the glass wall. They were on their hands and knees groping for something in a large rectangular tub of dark mossy water.

"I don't feel a thing," he said, shaking his head.

"It has to be in here," said the woman.

They were, Cable assumed, lab assistants—youngish, blondish, dressed in jeans, lab coats and sneakers.

The man noticed Cable and said, "Hi."

"Hi. Lose a contact lens?"

"Funny. Take a look, would you?" he asked her. "About in the middle. We dropped a cooper's digger."

The woman looked up at Cable and merely smiled; Cable thought she saw amusement in her eyes.

Cable pushed her sleeves up and knelt by the tub. A swampy odor rose from it, and there seemed to be little dead things floating on its surface. But if these two could put their hands in there, so could she. The water was cool.

"What is a cooper's digger—some kind of shovel?" she asked. She watched her hands disappear from sight in the murky liquid.

"Not exactly," he said. "Tell you what, if you'll make a disturbance there in the middle, it'll move toward one or the other of us."

Cable did as he suggested.

Suddenly the man jumped and grabbed something under water. "Gotcha," he said as he extracted a huge water rat with sleek black fur and angry red eyes. "Meet Alessandro," he said. "He's got a one-celled animal living in his fur that makes a terrific host."

Cable removed her hands from the water with deliberate slowness. "I'll remember that next time I throw a party," she quipped.

"Not bad," the man said with a chuckle. He patted the

squirming wet animal on the head to calm it and walked back to the lab.

The woman had a towel draped over one shoulder. She offered it to Cable, smiling apologetically. "You don't have to be crazy to be around him—"

"But it helps," said Cable. "I can see that." She extended a dry hand when she returned the towel. "I'm Alice Cable. New kid on the block. You guys part of Holland's crew?"

She laughed. "I'm Dr. Holland," she said.

Cable merely repeated, "You're Dr. Holland."

"Not *the* Dr. Holland. That was Alec who carried Alessandro away. I'm Linda. He's the brains in the family. I just cook up what he invents."

Alec Holland returned, drying his hands. "Don't believe her. She's got an IQ like a phone number." He took Cable's hand. "Hi," he said again.

"Hi," she said. She could not take her eyes from his face. She could not have explained why—only that everything she saw there she liked.

"I heard you say you have a sensor out," he said. "Number three?"

"Number three," she said. "I don't know how important it is, or what's wrong with it, but the display says it's malfunctioning."

"Want to take a look?"

Cable felt a confusion that kept her from thinking at her usual level of efficiency. "Uh, I suppose I could ask Charlie to give me an escort." She hoped she wasn't smiling.

"Maybe we could get your mother to come along, too," said Alec with a grin. He laughed at her frown. "The only dangerous thing out there is the Government Eagle Scouts and their popguns."

Linda said, "He exaggerates."

Alec said, "You *are* the Alice Cable who unscrambled the Venus surface maps when nobody at JPL could manage it, aren't you?"

She nodded, amused.

25

"The same Alice Cable who straightened out Dr. Haines's biochemical data at Princeton?"

"Amazing," she said.

"Then let's go look at sensor number three. I'll give you the Cook's Tour. Ritter's always after me to get some fresh air; he'll be tickled pink."

"I don't think Cook has swamp tours," Cable said.

"Then it's a Holland tour." He looked through the glass ceiling at the trace of sunlight that still rimmed the mossy old wall. "We have plenty of time to get there and back before dark."

The look on her face said: but why?

He answered, "I want to show you my world."

4

Ritter was nowhere in sight when Alec Holland hauled out the hidden blue coat and conscripted Bill Darkow to help carry it to the inlet.

"Ritter said he wanted the boat to stay hidden," Cable said, wondering what Alec's reply would be: it would tell a lot about him, she suspected, and help her understand Ritter's place here.

"You can't ride in a hidden boat," Alec said simply. "He worries too much."

The boat sloshed into the water.

"Keep an eye out for Sam," Bill requested. "He must be out there somewhere."

"Will do," said Alec as he pulled the starter of the outboard.

As they chugged slowly down the widening inlet, Alec tossed Cable a bottle of insect repellent. "Put a little on your face and hands," he suggested. "Mosquitos get desperate around sunset. Desperate and daring."

As the inlet widened, the cypress trees grew thicker and taller. Alec maneuvered slowly around the roots and trunks until the way ahead was open and sunlit. Then he fixed the rudder and leaned back in his seat. He opened his arms wide, as if to increase the area touched by the warm golden sunlight.

"You look like a tree," said Cable.

"I think like a tree sometimes," he said. "I know how they feel about sunlight and wind and rain and chills. See these cypresses? They're the happiest trees in the world."

"The happiest," she repeated, sort of understanding what he meant. "They tell you this?"

"In a way. They make sounds, you know, and they move." He noted her incredulous expression and became less fanciful. "Besides, how do you know when a *person* is happy? Certainly not when they tell you so. When they act like it."

"And the trees here act like it?"

"Are you blind, woman? Look around you. Look at teeming, successful life. Happy life."

Unguided, the boat entered the water of the wide shallow lake. A small flock of flamingos touched down along a distant shore; their color was electric pink in the hot light of the setting sun. A white waterbird dived from a great height, scooped into the lake and rose, carrying away a fish. A cloud of dragonflies buzzed across the path of the quiet boat. Unlike Charlie, Bill, Ritter, and the others she had met, Alec belonged here, was accepted here.

"Like the swamps?" he asked her.

She hesitated. "Hate swamps," she said finally. "Hate bugs. Hate things without legs."

He laughed. "You can't tell me this isn't beautiful."

"Well," she said, grinning, "yes, it's beautiful—at this very moment, at sunset, out in the open like this, with a guide I trust; but if I use a little imagination I could scare myself to death."

"Why'd you come?"

"For one thing, somebody specifically requested that I be sent. For another—" She cut herself off and let her subconscious complete a thought. "Were you the one who requested me?"

"Guilty," he said. "They didn't *make* you take the job, did they?"

"No." She did not feel like telling him more. Someday, perhaps, she would tell him how long his work, his career had fascinated her.

Alec reached back and angled the motor so that they made a wide turn and headed back toward the peninsula. He aimed for a point some distance from the church, toward the tip of the finger of land.

As the boat passed through a particularly shallow area, water plants scraped the bottom of the boat with a swishing sound.

Cable looked over the side. Strands of dead weed caught on the bow and then slid away; they looked like snakes. "Ugh," she said.

"Neatness freak, huh?"

She nodded. "You could eat off my kitchen floor."

He chuckled. "You could eat off this swamp. Maybe half the world could eat off this swamp, if only we knew how to manage the resources."

"Don't you know?"

"Everywhere I look I see mysteries. It's a pyramid. For every one thing I learn, I find two new questions."

"Electronics is like that." She laughed. "We could eat off the swamp, but it seems more likely that the swamp would like to eat us."

Alec shook his head, denying the dangers wordlessly.

"What happened to the guy I'm replacing, for instance?" she asked.

Alec sat up straight and said, a shade defensively, "Well, the guy stepped right on the gator's head. The gator only did what came naturally. Who do you blame for that? It's like wandering across the street in front of a bus, for God's sake."

She smiled. "You do love it here, don't you?"

"Yep."

His eyes were too intense; she felt she had to look away. Then she realized that was only part of the problem: she knew two things the others did not want her to mention to Alec, two things that would hurt him.

"What is it?" he probed, seeing something sad in her face.

She looked at the red sun sandwiched between orange and amber clouds. "Have you talked to Charlie about the grant?" she asked.

"Oh. I didn't need to. If the committee had renewed our support, Charlie would have said that instead of hello. That won't knock the props out from under me. I own part

29

of the lab, and there's money from other sources.''

She smiled. "If that won't do you in, maybe nothing else will, either. Why are you looking at me like that?"

"Like what?"

Like, Cable thought, you simply enjoy looking at me. "Oh, nothing," she said.

Alec slowed the engine further as he began to navigate the cypresses near the shore. The sun was almost down, and twilight had already reached the wooded land. Though they could not know it, Alec was threading his way along the exact route Sam Darkow had taken earlier in the afternoon.

It became noticeably dimmer as the boat drifted under thick festoons of hanging moss. The side of the boat scraped by a cypress root.

"Do we have a flashlight?" Cable asked.

"There's one in the tool kit under your seat. We shouldn't need it, though."

"I'm taking it anyway."

Alec helped her to firm land and led her along a narrow path through dense foliage. He moved swiftly; she stayed several steps behind him.

She paused once to look at her mud-caked feet. "I paid a fortune for these boots," she muttered.

He chuckled. "Better keep moving. There's a fair amount of quicksand along here."

At that moment they heard distant voices.

"Who's that?" Cable asked.

"I don't know," said Alec, his ear turned to the distance.

A twig snapped from somewhere much closer.

"Come on," Alec urged.

Cable pulled her sinking boot out of the mire with a huge sucking sound. "And I hate mud," she said.

"More than smog?" he asked wryly.

"Probably."

"Keep your eyes open," he said, as they hurried ahead, toward a brighter clearing in the trees.

"What for?" she asked, wide-eyed, apprehensively.

He bent low and scooped up a blossom that had been attached to a tree root. "One of these might jump out and get you."

As they came to a stop in the clearing he handed her the large wax-petaled flower.

"It's lovely," she said. As she turned it over in her hands, she absently wiped mud off her shoe on a gnarled root that seemed designed for that purpose.

"Look," Alec instructed. He gestured toward mounds of flowers that were still visible and vibrant in the twilight. "There are over a hundred species of genus *orchia* here, growing like dandelions."

"Happy orchids, too," she said with a chortle.

"Yes. Happy orchids. There's so much beauty in the swamps, if you open your eyes to it. *You* can't see beyond the chaos, the mess." He tapped her chest gently. "Look inside your own body, the most magnificent creation, and what do you see? Formica? Straight lines? Chrome and deodorant? Heck no, you see blood, bone, the pump and flow of a million messy miracles." He took the orchid and stored it in his shirt pocket.

"That's true . . . but I'm more cerebral, I guess. I don't live inside my body but inside my mind. No, that's not fair, you do too. What I mean is that I think in right angles, circuits, the logic of electron flows; okay—chromium and Formica. And I like an ordered world around me."

He stepped closer to her and said softly, suggestively, "Look at the most creative thing a man and woman can do, and you'll see things growing, unpredictable, magical . . . hot."

She pushed him away. "Save malarkey like that for your wife, Holland. Now, if you don't mind, where's that sensor?"

He laughed. "Right over there." He laughed again, as if the sensor were about to play some joke on her.

They heard rustling in the underbrush again. This time they glimpsed a man running, stumbling away from them.

"Who's there?" Alec called out. "Sam?"

The runner did not answer.

There was a shout from somewhere deep in the swamp.

"Who's there?" Alec called again.

Still there was no answer.

Cable had reached the sensor and had lifted the hemispherical rain hood off of it. The array of instruments was clustered around a core which was attached to the pole that held the sensor about five feet from ground level. "Alec," she said quietly. "Come look at this."

The wires connecting the modules had been cut. So had the lines to the telemetric transmitter.

"Why would anybody want to do that?" Cable asked.

Alec nodded. "I'm afraid I can imagine why someone might want to blind us and make us deaf. But who . . . when . . . and how did they get in and out unnoticed?"

"I'm not sure they were unnoticed. We may have just noticed one of them. Why wouldn't that guy answer?"

"Do you have any way of determining when this was cut?" he asked.

Cable nodded. "If your system is engineered the way I think it is, there's a built-in clock. I can tell you to the split second when this went off the air."

"Was this the only one showing malfunction?"

"I—I'm not sure. It's the only malfunction the computer *volunteered*; I didn't ask it if there were others." Cable was still looking at the damaged sensor. "I can fix this; but not tonight. It'll take a while."

Alec looked up to the dimming lavender in the sky. "We'd better get back," he said.

5

When they returned to the inlet, Alec and Cable found lights burning in the several shacks and beaming from the front church windows. The brightest stars were visible in the purple sky.

Alec slowed the boat, and Cable jumped out of it before it had completely stopped. She ran up the slope, to the bridge, toward the church—and stopped. Except for the lights burning, the camp seemed deserted. The stillness was eerie.

"Charlie?" she called out.

Alec secured the boat and ran to her side.

Charlie emerged from the command shed, Cable's cabin. "Cable," he called out, "where the hell have you been?"

"Charlie! Did anything suspicious happen while we were gone? Any strangers come into camp?"

The door to the church opened and Ritter stalked out. "You're damn right something suspicious happened," he said angrily. "A stupid broad of a technician, first day on the job, takes the scientist we're all supposed to be guarding on an unguarded romp in the bush! What kind of children's games to you think we're playing here, Cable?"

Alec stepped forward. "Now, look, Ritter, she had nothing to do with—"

"If I have my way," said Ritter, "and by God I will, you'll be on the next chopper back to Washington!"

Other guards had heard the shouting and were appearing out of curiosity.

"Calm down, Ritter," said Charlie. "How could she have known?"

Ritter wheeled on Holland. "Outside the lab, you've got no sense at all, Alec. How do we keep you away from women like this?"

Holland laughed, unable to take Ritter's tirade seriously. "I've never known a woman like this," he said lightly. "Have you?"

Cable said flatly, "There's a cut sensor out there. Deliberately cut."

"Which sector?" Ritter asked, his storm passing.

"Sector three," said Cable.

Ritter said, "Your predecessor was working on that one when he got chewed up by the gator." He spelled out for her, as if talking to a child: "Needless to say, he didn't have a chance to put it back together before we took him to the morgue."

Cable nodded, smiling sheepishly. "I see." Something still worried her.

What bothered Cable was the number of severed wires and the sloppy way they had been cut. Sensor three did not look as if someone had been at work on repairing it. It looked as if it had been sabotaged. But she knew it was difficult to second-guess the methods of another engineer—especially one under attack by an alligator.

Ritter seemed to want to say more to Cable, but he simply turned and walked away, toward the security headquarters shack.

"Sorry, Cable," Alec said.

"I thought you said Ritter would be tickled pink if you went out for a little fresh air," she said.

Charlie said, "Give him an hour or two; he'll cool down." The white-haired administrator took out a cigarette and started to light it. "You didn't see Sam Darkow out there, did you?"

"We saw somebody," Alec said, "but if it was Sam, he didn't answer us. Is he still missing?"

"I'm afraid we have to look at it that way now. He's missing. Bill's out looking for him in the other boat." His face flickered in the yellow light from the match he cupped in his hands. "Probably nothing to worry about.

Probably just dropped his walkie-talkie in the soup and will show up here any minute.''

Cable studied Charlie Thaxton for an instant. Something in his voice said he was worried and he cared. It occurred to her that Charlie—bred to be a desk-bound Washington administrator—loved it here, felt attached to the importance of the work being done, wished he were more a part of it, more an adventurer.

The match went out. Charlie slowly crushed it and dropped it to the ground.

If she were right about Charlie, then he was more concerned about Arcane rumors than he had let on. She remembered his reluctance to tell Alec the rumor, or the truth about the withdrawn funds; and she added to her new picture of Charlie the fact that openness was not one of his cardinal virtues.

Alec must have been having similar thoughts—he knew Charlie better, after all—for he stepped over to the white-haired man and laid a hand on his shoulder. "Not much more we can do about Sam tonight," he said. "Bill will find him. Let's go to the lab and drink a toast to persevering on our own, with less money."

Charlie brightened. "You know—"

"You must be terrible at poker, Charlie. No wonder they don't want you loose around Washington."

"They want your substance, too," Charlie said, relieved to be able to talk about it.

"So—we'll send 'em a generous sample. Big deal.''

Cicadas had taken over the sounds of the evening; their shrill vibrations were constant and piercing.

Suddenly there were four quick retorts, like gunshots. They came from the church.

The guard opened the wide church doors; they heard a scream. It was Linda's voice.

"Dr. Holland!" the guard called frantically, unnecessarily; Alec, Charlie and Cable were already running toward the lab.

The security door was standing open; two guards, their pistols drawn, stood just inside the lab.

Linda Holland stood there alone with a silly grin on her face. "Sorry," she said inadequately. She was holding a beaker of fluorescent yellow liquid.

"Thanks, guys," Alec said to the guards, dismissing them.

When they were gone, and the door was sealed once more, Alec tipped his head inquisitively at Linda, who still grinned strangely.

"The damndest thing," Linda began, shaking her head in disbelief, "this newest batch you had me cook up." She dipped her fingertips gently into the liquid. "I knew we'd formulated something revolutionary, but this is literally dynamite. Watch."

She flicked her fingers over the bare floor; several drops sailed from her fingertips and exploded with a bright green flash where they struck. The wooden flooring flared briefly into ordinary smoke and fire—which died down to leave small, round charred areas.

"Dr. Holland?" a startled guard called through the closed lab door.

"It's all right," he yelled back. To Linda, he said, "That's incredible. Why should that much energy be released?"

"Weird, huh?" said Linda.

Alec knelt to examine the charred spots; he rubbed charcoal onto his fingertips and felt the consistency of the powder. He laughed—for reasons obscure to Cable and Charlie.

Charlie said, "Wonderful. You've reinvented nitro. For this we've fed the mosquitos for ten months? If the taxpayers only knew, Alec. If the poor bastards only knew."

Alec chuckled; "You'll find a way to break it to them gently, Charlie."

Charlie shook his head in mock consternation. "You people will be up all night, no doubt, testing this—whatever it is, right?"

"I wouldn't be surprised," said Alec.

"You can give me a report at breakfast," Charlie said as

he reached for the wall panel that opened the security door. "Good luck," he added as the door shut him away from the scientists.

Charlie stood for a long moment staring at that door, that token of modern technology—a door with the built-in judgment to know whom to admit and whom to reject. He was thinking that it was minds—people—like the three in that lab who had given and would continue to give all such marvels to the world. At other times he knew better, but now he wondered what possible good he was doing the world: compared to progress and invention, of what value were government and diplomacy? Compared to this small hidden laboratory in no-man's land, of what significance was Washington, D.C.?

As he turned and left the church, he said to himself, in a rare moment of total honesty, "That's why I've never made much of myself: I don't believe in my own importance." He shook the heavy thought away in an instant; if it ever came up again, he knew, he'd have ample rationales to diminish the truth of it.

The cicadas were even louder now, and bullfrogs were agitated in the hot night air. Charlie heard a splash down the inlet. A fish breaking the surface? A bird diving? An alligator leaving the bank?

Bright floods lighted the clearing and the fronts of the shacks. Voices came from Cable's quarters. Charlie walked toward the sound; he recognized Ritter's voice. He assumed that the security chief was making a cursory check of the remote sensors, seeing if more than number three was out.

Efficient man, Ritter, thought Charlie; efficient, crude, dedicated, malevolent and violent. It was difficult to imagine why the man attached himself so to the welfare of the Hollands. Perhaps, thought Charlie, he's one of those duty-above-all cop types.

The light in the shack went out and the door creaked open.

For some vague reason, Charlie did not wish to be seen; he stepped behind the broad trunk of a pine tree.

Ritter and one of his men came out. Ritter was laughing at something as he slammed the door behind him and in the same sweeping gesture slapped the rusty chain of the porch swing.

"What time is it?" Ritter asked his companion.

The young man pressed the light on his watch and said, "Early yet; eight fifty-three."

"Did you get Holland's boat back under the camouflage?"

"Yes, sir."

The two walked across the clearing and into the guard house.

Charlie leaned against the tree for a moment and then stepped to Cable's porch. He reached for the door, knowing it might be locked. Ritter kept a pass key, but Charlie did not.

The door opened easily, with a loud creak.

Charlie stepped inside. He decided that he really did not need light; he could see the instruments well enough by moonlight. He switched off the lamps on the master circuit and threw the switch. Transformers buzzed faintly as myriad signal lights winked on; the instruments pertaining to security—the ones Ritter had evidently just consulted—came to life.

"SENSOR OUT/SECTOR THREE," the disaply still announced.

Charlie studied the keyboard and thought he remembered a thing or two about the use of it. He typed in SCAN and hit the start button.

SENSOR OUT/SECTOR FIVE.

The screen went blank, then:

SENSOR OUT/SECTOR NINE.

Sectors ten, eleven and twelve were also out. As security measures, the perimeter sensors were useless. No alarms would go off.

Why had Ritter been laughing, Charlie wondered suddenly. He must not have checked the system after all. Or maybe that wasn't the answer.

Charlie turned to the camera monitors. Four infrared

video cameras were trained on the principal access routes leading to camp; Charlie activated their powerful zoom lenses. The night photography with its highly exaggerated contrast took some getting used to. Charlie had to use his imagination to separate the moonlight on tree trunks from the moonlight on streams and inlets. The image was more a result of heat than of visible light.

Not far from camp, on a path one might take to reach or return from sector three, something on the ground glowed. Charlie zoomed in on it. He felt almost certain it was a man's body—a living body, judging by the heat radiating from it.

Sound was arriving from one of the few working sensors —in sector six, several miles from the body. It was Bill Darkow's voice calling for his brother.

Charlie thought. The body on the path could very well be Sam Darkow.

The radio on the table before him might be able to contact Bill, if he carried a walkie-talkie. It would also contact anyone else listening; and Charlie was somehow convinced that that would not be a good idea.

He left the instruments operating and ran from the shack. It occurred to him briefly to tell Alec what he was doing, but clearly a life might depend upon his reaching that body as quickly as possible.

Charlie ran until his middle-aged heart was thudding in his chest. Just as he feared he'd have to slow to a walk, he saw the body in the path ahead of him. He'd been right; it was Sam Darkow. He was lying on his back, his eyes closed, his clothes and skin dripping with sweat.

"Sam!" Charlie said, drooping to his knees. He tried to rouse him by moving his head.

The young man's eyes opened slowly, and his lips parted.

Charlie stood and called out, instinctively, incautiously, "Bill! Can you hear me? I've found him!"

"No!" Sam said weakly. "Quiet."

"What happened, Sam? Can you walk if I help you?" Charlie asked as he knelt down again.

Sam said, "Don't think so." He tried to lift an arm, and it was barely evident to Charlie that that's what he was doing; he couldn't lift it off the ground. "Cottonmouth," Sam said in a whisper. "Deliberate. Ferret. Men."

"Ferret?" Charlie asked, not sure whether Sam meant a man or a thing.

The ferns to the side of the trail rustled, and a dark shape emerged. "Yes," it said in a rough voice, "Ferret." Moonlight glinted from his gold earring and the white of his teeth.

Four other men, slightly smaller men, stepped out of the underbrush and stood near their master.

6

When Charlie left the lab ("Good luck," he had said as the door hissed shut) Alec said to Cable and Linda:

"I think we've *had* our good luck; now we've got to get to work!"

Cable noted enviously how effectively Alec and Linda worked together. He took the beaker from Linda, whisked it to a workbench crowded with implements and glass containers; she immediately went to a wall safe and took out a worn notebook.. Alec pulled up two tall stools, one for himself, another for Linda, while she took several chemicals—the ones she knew he'd want—from a shelf. Together, they were as efficient as a machine.

Cable's instinct was to leave them to their work. She headed for the door.

"Hey, don't go," Alec said to her. "This is going to be exciting! At least, I think it is. Pull up a stool."

When Cable spoke she did not like the accusing tone she heard in her own voice, but there was nothing she could do about it. "I *thought* you had to be working on some sort of weapon system. I didn't think all this security was to protect a lot of—"

"Plants?" Alec finished. "But that *is* what it's for. The only way I ever expected my work to be explosive was socially. We just developed this formula last week. We haven't even tested it beyond microscopic analysis; so give me a break."

"Okay," she said, smiling.

"Look around. Let me get started, and then I'll tell you what we're doing." From his pocket he took the orchid he had picked in sector three, and set it on the desk in front of him. He said to it, "Been a rough day for all of us, hasn't it?" It was wilted and crushed.

Cable looked around. As a scientist, Alec might be precise as a printed circuit, but in other ways he was evidently as messy as his swamp. The railing of the sleeping balcony above was draped with jeans and shirts, and Cable saw the end of an unmade bed. Among the centrifuges, spectroscopes, heaters and refrigerators on the lab racks there was a stereo player with a dusty disc ignored on the turntable. Albums on the shelf below were filed unevenly, and she glanced at them to verify her suspicion that they would not be in any intelligible order. She thought of her own collection—all in new plastic sleeves and in alphabetical order. It would have been nice if she could have liked him less for his sloppiness; unfortunately, it did not affect her feelings at all. There were two discarded pairs of sneakers on a table piled high with scraps and parts of instruments. There were no women's things in sight. Linda was neater.

Although instrumentation was a specialty of Cable's, there were machines here she had never seen before—some simple, some peculiarly complex. Like the array of modules at which Alec began to labor. She moved closer to watch him.

"You like gadgets," he observed. "Bet you never saw this kind of electron scope before. Made it myself."

Her eye went immediately to an open box of circuit work. Messy, at first glance, clean but chaotic on closer inspection.

"You ought to put a cover on that," she said.

"I've got one for it somewhere," he said, unconcerned.

The video display of the scope faded on. The supermagnified image there looked like a lunar landscape. He turned knobs, and faint colors—pink, green, brown— tinted the shapes.

"Holland," she said with a touch of exasperation, "what are you doing? I mean, it's time: tell me what this lab is all about."

Alec appeared to ignore her; he concentrated on tuning the scope before him. As he turned dials and flipped micro-switches, the image was sharpened, enhanced, intensified. The picture began to move, to pan right to left, and the "terrain" changed.

42

"Ignore that first picture," he told her. "It's just imperfections in the glass slide. I know, I know, I ought to be neater."

"This isn't a transmission-type scope," Cable observed.

"No, sort of a scanner."

"What's the order of magnification?"

"What you're seeing is seventy thousand times. By the way, don't touch anything. We're using thirty thousand volts—which isn't all that powerful for a scope, but it'll kill you."

"I thought I saw the lights dim."

"All over camp. Everybody knows when we're magnifying."

The picture became smooth, showing an unpitted surface, and into view came a cluster of segmented organisms. Like round tape worms. Alec sharpened the image further.

"Ah," he said, satisfied. "See these little guys here? They're DNA chromosomes from the common lab bacilli *E. Coli.*" He typed an instruction into the computer keyboard at his side. "Now hold that picture in your mind."

The screen went black as he carefully removed the carrier that held the slide that held the specimen; he replaced it with another, and quickly focused in on it. "This is another common bacilli, a plant matrix called D complex."

After typing further instructions for his extraordinary microscope, he leaned back and waited for the machine to do his bidding. "Each of those organisms has been around labs for years," he remarked. Again he removed the slide and inserted a third. While he was doing this, the image processor displayed a split-screen picture, the segmented *E. coli* on the left and the rod-shaped D complex on the right. "There's nothing unusual about either of these— except that one is animal and the other is vegetable."

The split-screen picture dissolved into the contents of the third slide: a segmented *E. coli* with dark, rod-like spurs from D complex grafted onto it.

While she watched, Cable saw one of the organisms twitch.

This sample was alive.

Alec tapped the screen like a proud father. "This is the new guy. He's never existed before on the face of the earth. A basic vegetable cell with an animal nucleus." Alec turned on his stool to face Cable. He smiled at her wide-open mouth. "A plant," he continued, "with an animal's aggressive power of survival. If we can do it on this scale, we can do it on any scale—algae to trees. A plant for the twenty-first century."

She turned from the screen to look at Alec. "Recombinant DNA. But I never thought—"

"You've read about it?"

"Yes, I—I've followed your career rather closely. I know enough about the subject to be awed, and scared. What are you after—tomatoes the size of weather balloons?"

Linda arrived with a newly prepared slide. As Alec inserted it in the microscope, he said to Cable, "I wouldn't mind having tomatoes that would grow in a desert, or orange trees for the Arctic, or vegetables that would grow like weeds in depressed countries, say, by 2001 when there'll be six-and-a-half billion people on this planet, most of them hungry."

Alec spoke so matter-of-factly that Cable realized she had never seen him so solemn. Her eye now made sense of a Xerox photo she had half-noticed; it was stuck to the back of the microscope. A child—a child ravaged by famine, with wide, wet eyes.

Alec grinned. "I'm no crusader, Cable."

"Yes, you are," she said softly.

He shook his head. "I want truth. Power over nature. I want to know we've left no stone unturned, no secret unexamined, in our drive to put ourselves and our universe to good use." He nodded toward the pathetic little girl. "She says to me, 'Look a little harder, Alec; you're so close to the answer."

Alec drummed his fingers on the CRT display. "Here's one of those answers . . . I think. If this stuff works—and it'll be a long time before we know—it will make, well, a little difference. To me. And to her."

Linda bent over and kissed him on the cheek.

Cable felt a nagging unease inside that continued to make her argumentative. She felt a bit like a debate defending a position she did not believe in. "If it would alter plants so drastically, what would it do to animals? To people?"

"I wasn't planning to market it as a new soft drink."

"Maybe not you, but what if it fell into the wrong hands?"

"What wrong hands?" he asked. "That's boogey-man mentality. 'Somehow' thinking. We're a long way from having to worry about control of it. It might turn out to be as safe and common as garden fertilizer. A dozen brands. Buy it at your local hardware and nursery." He chuckled. "Nothing wrong with you, Cable, that a few months without television won't cure. Television makes people paranoid hypochondriacs. What if the worst happens to *you?* —That kind of thing. That's why I haven't wanted any publicity. If people get worried before there's anything to worry about, they have the power to put the brakes on the development of everything worthwhile."

Linda had been watching the CRT display with fascination. "Alec. Look at that!" she said. "The new formula —it's replicating like mad!"

The display showed a writhing tangle of rods and segments that moved erratically, energized by the miraculous medium they found themselves in. The cells divided— unzipped like animated DNA demonstrations Cable had seen—and recombined in a random order that resulted in many animal/vegetable cells. Incredibly, in the short time the scientists watched, one of the new combination cells itself divided into identical combined offspring.

"Good lord!" said Linda.

Alec dittoed her sentiment with a nod. His mouth had been dangling open; he closed it with a click of his teeth. "Let's try it on something," he suggested. He held the beaker of yellow fluid up to the light. "I just put that microbe from Alessandro's fur in here for the heck of it. Do you suppose that triggered accelerated growth?" He answered his own question, "No, it couldn't have." He walked to another workbench, placed the beaker in a rack there, and returned with the shriveled orchid.

"Looks like the plants in my apartment," Cable muttered. "I may be neat, but everything I water dies."

Cable watched as Alec scrupulously measured the solution and reported to note-taker Linda: "One part formula to one hundred parts water."

Linda glanced at her watch and included time and date with her notes. "Anything special about the flower?" she asked.

"Just call it a cut orchid blossom, damaged but recently bloomed, stem about thirteen and a half centimeters." He dropped the orchid into the beaker of preparation and carefully, tenderly, set it—a decoration—on a round wooden table. Cable suspected the table served as a dining table when it was needed for that.

Her eyes wandered up the bookshelves to the glass grid of a ceiling. She saw, through the naked beams of the old church roof, several bright stars and a gibbous moon. A small meteor streaked across the sky.

"Did you see that?" she asked.

"What?" Alec asked absently.

Cable realized suddenly that nothing as mundane as a shooting star would compete with this exotic yellow liquid that had just been fed to the orchid. "Nothing," she said, sloughing the matter aside. "How long before you'll see some effect?"

Alec tore his blank stare away from the orchid and looked at Cable. "Do you expect it to leap out of its pot and dance a fandango? It could take a week or longer."

Somehow, she wanted to hurt him, wanted to hurt this man she considered a courageous and benevolent genius. Before she could talk herself out of it, she said caustically, "Your work has all the thrills of watching grass grow."

He said angrily, "There's nothing much more thrilling than watching grass grow." He took the notebook from Linda and slapped it shut as he crossed the lab to the wall safe and then tossed it in.

"Ooops," Cable said.

Linda shrugged and said, "Forget it. Despite his jokes he's ridiculously sensitive. I suppose I should have warned you. Our dad was the same—religious about his work."

Cable wasn't sure she heard properly. "Your dad?"

Linda said, "Haven't you ever heard of Walter Holland, the biophysicist? Nobel Prize?"

"Oh, yes, I've heard of him, but I thought—"

"He used to throw a mean bunsen burner, I can tell you. His temper flared so suddenly. Alec and I spent half our childhood cleaning up after his tantrums. Perfectionist till the day he died. Alec's the same—only he doesn't usually throw things." Linda had been speaking casually, unaware of the startled expression on Cable's face. She turned to switch off the various instruments associated with the electron microscope. With the last switch, the room lights brightened noticeably.

Cable looked at Alec's back and said to herself: *Playing a little game, were we, Dr. Holland?* She asked Linda in a whisper, "Is he married?"

Linda shook her head with a smile that seemed to say: *He's all yours; but are you sure you know what you're asking for?* She said, "Excuse me for a minute or two; I'm going to wash up and call it a day. Join us for supper, why don't you? One of the twins bagged some wild turkey and dressed one for us. You can help me figure out how to cook it."

Cable laughed. "That *will* be a challenge. I'm not much of a cook."

"Alec's a whiz in the kitchen. He'll help," Linda said, as she disappeared behind one of the towering bookshelves. Cable heard a door shut on the other side.

"Oh, my God," Alec said suddenly in an intense quiet voice. "My God, my God . . . ."

Cable looked over by the wall safe and saw Alec staring at the floor.

"What is it?" Cable asked, alarmed by the shock in his voice.

"Look," he said.

47

She stood beside him and saw what he saw. Five bright green shoots, two to three feet high, had sprouted out of the floorboards. It seemed to have happened without benefit of sun, water, nourishment or time. They were walnut saplings—new and healthy.

Alec bent to the floor, knelt, then sat on the hard, dead wood. "Cable, I don't believe this! They're still growing. You can watch them!" He reached out his hand and touched a bud as it unfurled into a leaf.

"Jesus," Cable whispered, "you *can* see them grow!" She sat beside him and reached out to touch one of the sprouts—as if to convince herself it was real.

Alec said, "The places where Linda threw the drops of formula. Look, you can see the charred marks around the bases of the stems."

Cable gasped. "Of course! Alec, it's fantastic!"

The two of them had a thought simultaneously; the orchid had been soaking in the solution of formula. Both leapt to their feet and ran to the dining table.

Instead of the crushed, withered thing that had been there before, now there was a plant that was thickly leaved with an enormous, flawless bloom and a powerful, wiry root that had found its way out of the beaker and wrapped around the table so powerfully that the wood's veneer was buckled.

Alec stared at it, transported. "I *don't* believe this!" *He* yelled, "Linda! Get in here quick!"

While they watched, the beaker cracked; the trunk had grown too fat for it. A splinter sprang out of the strained tabletop.

Alec grabbed Cable and kissed her. It was at first meant to be a fleeting gesture, but it held; Cable kissed him back.

"What is it?" Linda asked excitedly. "Oh," she said when she saw them, "I hope you weren't expecting to surprise me." Then she saw the orchid, and her mouth dropped.

"And look!" Alec said pointing at the shoots rising from the floor. They were now nearly as tall as Linda.

Linda yanked open a wide metal drawer under a workbench. "Take measures, clippers, scalpel, slides for samples—what else do I need?"

"Get the notebook back out of the safe."

Cable asked, "Can I do anything?"

Alec chuckled, allowing himself the luxury of taking his mind off work for a second. He said, "I bet you can do anything you set your mind to, Cable."

"I've generally found that to be true," she said with a grin.

"I want Charlie to see this—because he's a friend—and Ritter, because the bastard's always acted as if we're somehow throwing his money away. Want to go get them?"

"Sure," said Cable. She hurried to the door.

"Hell," said Alec, "I feel like busting that damn security door down so the whole world can come take a look!"

Cable considered the spirit of his remark and answered seriously, "I don't think that would be a great idea, Alec. Not yet."

She left them and ran out into the night.

It was dark. For some reason, the floodlights that had illuminated the camp earlier were not burning.

7

Cable stopped short. The only light she saw came from her own quarters. Probably just Charlie or Ritter, she thought; maybe both. Checking the perimeter sensors.

The night sounds of the swamp were, oddly, both frightening and tranquilizing—the piping of treefrogs, bullfrogs croaking in the tall sawgrass by the bridge, the ringing of a million insects. She began to make her way across the dark clearing.

She tripped over a loop of sassafras root, stumbled but did not fall. Her eyes were adjusting to the moonlight. She saw someone standing in the middle of the clearing—a big man, a rifle under his arm. "Hello," she called ahead to him.

He did not answer; he did not move.

He was huge, with arms like those of a circus strong man. In the moonlight his face looked smooth, boyish. She was sure she had not seen him before. She asked him, "Is Ritter back? And do you know where Charlie is?"

The man looked at her oddly, and for a moment she wondered if he spoke English. He gestured toward her shack and said, "Go to the the command shed, miss." He gave her half a salute.

"What's your name?"

"Bruno, miss." He looked away, not interested in her.

"Thanks," she said with a shrug. "Why are the floodlights out?" she asked as an afterthought.

"I don't know," he said.

As she approached the command shed she wondered if Alec's use of the powerful microscope had blown a fuse or a generator. "Charlie?" she called when she reached the porch. "You there?" There was no answer. "Ritter?"

The screen door screeched open and banged shut. She saw no one inside. The sounds of night were diminished indoors, and the hum of instruments—all operating—blended with the swamp noises like some new breed of insect. Apart from the instruments, only one lamp burned.

"Who left everything running?" she wondered aloud. She was nervous. She half-expected someone to answer her.

She looked at the displays. The monitor was flashing a series of messages. *"SENSOR OUT/SECTOR THREE"* turned into *"SENSOR OUT/SECTOR FOUR"* which gave way to *"SENSOR OUT/SECTOR FIVE,"* and so on. The only operating sensors, according to the repeating cycle of messages, were one, two, and six.

Hair stirred on the back of Cable's neck. She knew, almost with certainty, that the sensors had been deliberately cut—that the camp was in some quiet way under attack.

She noted a blinking red light and the label under it: "Penetration." But she did not yet know the system well enough to guess where defenses had been penetrated.

There was an infrared picture on the video monitor. It wasn't just dark lines and shapes. It looked like two men lying on the ground. One of the bodies was brighter than the other—hotter. She sat at the workbench.

Her hand shaking, she operated the zoom control to enlarge the image as much as possible. One of the men had white hair. Neither was moving.

Cable reached for the shortwave. She switched it on and grabbed for the microphone. It came away in her hand; its cord was severed. She stared at the cord in disbelief.

She didn't hear him, although the man had to have been standing behind her near the door, waiting. He grabbed her arm and violently yanked her out of the chair, slung her around until she slammed into a wall.

51

Dazed, she slid to the floor, watching him lift the heavy radio and smash it like a watermelon against the workbench.

The man was surprisingly strong for someone so emaciated; he was enraged for no visible reason, terrifying. His eyes and his mouth were open wide, and he wore a gold earring.

He swooped down to grab Cable again, but she scrambled to her feet and out of his way. She ran for the door.

He caught her easily and hauled her at a run back through the cabin, into the small galley at the back.

She screamed as he spun her around and raised his arm to strike her. Instinctively she raised an arm to stop the blow and he grabbed her wrist, laughing gutturally. Miraculously she remembered her training in self-defense —training she had never had to put to the test—and she knew to push toward him instead of pulling away. With all her strength, she smashed her head straight into the bridge of his nose.

He reeled back, stunned, clutching his face. This gave Cable the time she needed to search for a weapon. She swept a propane fuel tank off the kitchen stove and whirled it through the air into the side of her attacker's head. There was a tremendous ringing concussion, and the man staggered and fell over a chair.

Cable made it out the door of the cabin.

The big man she had spoken to before no longer stood there in the moonlight. She had a hunch she could not trust him anyway. She ran toward the guard house but stopped short: the bodies of two guards lay face down in the high grass near the shack.

"Alec!" she screamed, but she knew that he would be unlikely to hear her. She yelled for him again and again as she ran toward the church.

A lumbering shape stepped out of the shadow of the church facade and stopped her the way a tree stops a runaway car. The wind was knocked out of her, but Bruno was off balance, too; and as she bounced off him her legs tripped him and the two fell together.

She got to her feet, and instead of entering the church she ran back to the guard house.

Another of Ferret's men charged at her from the darkness, chased her, but was not fast enough to stop her before she reached the bodies of the guards and pulled away an automatic rifle. She squeezed the trigger—three sharp shots—and the mercenary tumbled backward. Flocks of sparrows rustled out of trees into the black sky. Cable turned her sights on Bruno.

'Hold it!'' she ordered.

''I'm holding,'' said Bruno, skidding to a stop. ''I'm holding.'' He dropped his revolver and raised his hands.

She had to get to the church, and Bruno was still in the way. ''Back off,'' she instructed as she circled him, the rifle aimed from her hip.

''Drop it,'' growled a voice behind her. She felt the barrel of a gun hard against her back and saw a dozen more mercenaries coming at her from the shadows.

Her ears were ringing—not from the sounds of the swamp but from a dread screaming through her bloodstream; her legs tingled. The camp had been massacred, she assumed, except for herself and the Hollands. Charlie had to be dead. Ritter. All his men.

''Arcane,'' she said to her captor, the gray scarecrow with the earring.

He laughed. ''The name's Ferret,'' he said, his lips curling back like a wild animal's. ''Thinking can get you in trouble. It's going to get you killed, in fact.'' He laughed again—an angry, forced, mirthless sound.

She had lowered but not dropped the automatic. One of Ferret's men took it from her, cautiously, with a jerk; and two others grabbed her arms painfully.

''Take her along,'' said Ferret contemptuously; ''we'll need a key.''

They marched her, half-carrying, half-dragging her, through the double doors of the church.

A green-shaded ceiling fixture burned brightly; the big generator purred; the guard there lay on the floor, a knife protruding from his ribs, his dead eyes open.

"Your right hand, I think," Ferret said as he lifted it and aimed it at the fingerprint slot of the security lock. "Pretty hand," he said approvingly; "useful hand." He thrust it in. "I wonder if it has to be attached to work?"

She struggled, tried to curl her fingers; but she heard the solenoid *thunk* that signaled the motors to pull back the door.

"Alec!" she screamed. "Look out!"

Ferret cracked the butt of his .45 across Cable's skull, and she fell unconscious to the floor.

Alec and Linda had heard the three bursts from Cable's automatic. The sounds had been remote, but clearly gunshots. The scientists were absorbed so utterly by their new discoveries that the barest excuse had satisfied: Linda had said, "Another turkey shoot." And they had bent back over their notes and test tubes, wherein their minds dwelled like astral travelers, apart from the world the rest of humanity inhabits.

If they heard Cable yell before the door opened, it was no more than another of the animal sounds of the night, perhaps a blue heron taking to the air.

The door hissing open could not mean anything important.

The men standing there with guns were not real at first; then Alec's mind was wrenched back, shocked back to reality.

Ferret's wide, almost lidless eyes were on the orchid. It had continued to grow; its roots now crawled over and gripped the whole table. The table itself had sent tiny shoots into the air where the formula had spilled onto it from the broken beaker.

Linda moved close and gripped her brother's arm.

"Interesting specimen, Dr. Holland," said Ferret. "I'm sure I've never seen anything quite like it." He stepped toward it. "How long did this take to grow—a few days?

Does it live up to expectations, do you think, Doctor?"

Ferret viciously broke petals off the huge bloom and closed his fist around the stem.

Alec lurched forward automatically, enraged; but he was pushed back by the barrels of half-a-dozen guns.

Ferret tugged at the plant but could not dislodge it from the misshapen table. He lifted the table into the air, using the orchid stem as a handle. The plant seemed made of steel.

"Phenomenal!" Ferret squawked. "You're to be congratulated—if not rewarded. Phenomenal. Phenomenal." He dropped the table with a bang.

"What do you want?" Alec asked dully.

Ferret smiled; it was an ugly smile that did not reach his eyes. He looked around approvingly, admiringly, even up to the living quarters on the balconies above, up to the glass ceiling and the starry sky beyond. Alec had the nonsensical notion that this villian was about to announce: *It's simple, Dr. Holland, I want to be* you.

But Ferret said, "I represent a private party that wants your formula so badly they will give an arm and a leg for it." He leaned against one of the posts supporting a balcony. "You can make a successful deal if you're imaginative; even keep your life, if you're lucky."

Alec frowned, his thoughts racing, tumbling uselessly over one another. He shook his head.

Ferret said, "They're willing, however, to give *your* arm and leg—if necessary." He pointed his pistol at Alec's face. "You won't be given a few days to think this over."

"Get out of my lab," Alec said flatly.

Ferret cocked the gun. "The formula," he said grimly.

"Why?" Alec asked. "What do you want with it?"

Ferret shook his head. "Perhaps you don't have the imagination we credited you with, Dr. Holland."

Linda moved closer. "Alec," she said in a low voice, "the door."

Ritter stood there. He was silently surveying the situation. His pistol was drawn, and he seemed to be awaiting a chance to move, to turn the tables. Alec tried to conceal the feeling of hope he was afraid might show on his face, and he looked away from Ritter, wondering frantically how he might increase Ritter's chances, stall for time, diminish the odds against Ritter's one gun.

"The notebooks," Alec began, "they're . . . if I give them to you, you'll kill us."

"If you don't," said Ferret, "we'll kill you and tear this place apart."

"They're upstairs," Alec lied. Perhaps he could divide the troops.

"Now what would they be doing up there?" Ferret asked cynically. "Why wouldn't they be in the wall safe by the bookshelves?"

"How do you know—?"

Ritter stepped forward, slipping his gun into his belt. "What's the holdup?" he asked curtly.

Ferret said, "He's being difficult."

Linda gasped and Alec held her tighter.

"Ritter," said Alec, "not *you!* You have every security clearance I ever heard of." Alec studied the man now as he had not done before; he was dressed in black, a costume for concealment, an expensive velour utterly out of character for Ritter—a man of strictly practical tastes.

"No, Dr. Holland, not Ritter," the man said with a shrug. "Ritter, poor fellow, is long dead." He smiled from some secret joke. He grabbed his right ear and tugged; a mask began to stretch and peel away. "Actually," he said, "I've rather enjoyed this masquerade." His voice was becoming deeper, more cultured. "It's been quite a challenge for me to exhibit so little interest in your actual work here—which, in fact, I find extraordinary, revolutionary, almost as exciting, I dare say, as you do, Alec."

The mask was off, and the face beneath that of the pedestrian Ritter was sharp-featured, hawklike, conspicuously intelligent. As the man continued to speak, his voice continued to deepen until it sounded omnipotent, almost

56

benign; and the lumbering, tense posture of Ritter gave way to a straight spine, making of the man a taller, prouder, more imposing figure. There was a chilling electricity about him that in others might have been comforting, but in him was terrifying—out of context with his army of criminals. Insane.

"Our lawyers have become acquainted on occasion," he said with amusement, "but we've never met, officially. I won't offer my hand, because I'm quite confident you'd decline to shake it. My name is Arcane."

8

Arcane stared at Alec with a patient smile. "I'll give you a moment to review your predicament," he said. "I'd like us to work together, of course. If that doesn't appeal to you, the onus of an alternative falls on you. Your move."

"Where's Cable?" Alec asked.

"Outside. Alive at the moment." Impatiently, Arcane said, "You're not dealing with essentials, Alec."

"The electronics man who was killed by the alligator . . . that wasn't an accident," Alec stated with very little questioning inflection.

Ferret interjected gleefully. "It wasn't even an alligator."

"The man was a trifle too interested," said Arcane, "in field work. I'm waiting."

Alec's mind was a jumble of horrifying possibilities: Arcane finding ways to use the formula as a weapon, introducing commercial substances from untested byproducts, cornering the produce market, enslaving hungry countries with handouts, perhaps even causing ecological imbalances that could destroy the world—or holding the world for ransom with that threat.

Alec's eyes were on the orchid; while he stared at it a new leaf curled out and a blossom bud began to form. In spite of his situation, he wondered, as a scientist, how long the prodigious growth would continue before more nutrient was required, and what might happen when that time was reached. Or would it ever be reached? Would the plant/animal cells replicate themselves indefinitely? Would they be passed along to offspring?

Arcane took the pistol from his belt. This was not the

army-issue revolver Ritter had carried; Arcane's was gleaming, silver-plated.

"I'm waiting," Arcane said.

Alec made no response.

Linda said, "For God's sake, Alec, don't—"

Her brother cut her off by squeezing her close. "Shh," he said.

Arcane said to Ferret: "*Your* mistake, you see, was in threatening the great Dr. Holland. You don't know him. You make the silly mistake of suspecting that everyone's motives are the same, and that he'd react the way you would." Arcane shook his head. "What's called for here," he said, "is that we threaten the life of those he loves."

Arcane aimed his pistol at Linda's head; Ferret jumped out of the line of fire. "Whether we kill you or not, Alec, you have my word that when we leave the swamp, Linda will be alive. If she tries to tell her story she'll be locked in an asylum, but she'll be alive. I'm not afraid of witnesses, dear boy, because as you know, I'm dead." He snorted. "Died in a tragic accident."

"Don't believe him," Linda said weakly. "Don't do it."

Arcane moved closer to her. "Alec—give me the beaker of soup, the cultures used in its preparation, the chemicals of the medium, and your notes on the development. Or Linda dies now. Wouldn't that be a tragedy?"

Alec pulled away from his sister.

"No, Alec," she implored. "He'll kill us anyway."

Alec shrugged. "And find what he wants when we're dead."

"But maybe," said Arcane, "I'm more to be trusted than you imagine. You have that chance, you see. I advise you to avail yourself of it."

Alec's head was beginning to ache; there seemed to be no proper course of action, no step he could take without betraying all he cared about and believed in. He ran a clammy palm across his furrowed brow. "I'll get it," he said.

He left Linda beside the giant orchid, almost hoping its magical properties would protect her, and stepped to the wall safe.

It wasn't locked; he never locked it. He always assumed the space-age lock on the only entrance was enough protection for him and Linda and their secrets.

Bruno, baby-faced and bulbously over-muscled, followed Alec with a cocked revolver. He had to lower the firing pin and pocket it when Alec handed him the stack of notebooks. Bruno glanced inside the safe to see that none were being left behind.

"Fine," said Arcane. "Now the solution itself."

Alec nodded. A feeble plan had hatched in his brain. It was not a grandstand play, and in the long run it might make little or no difference, but it was something to try. With even so small a hint of purpose, his mind cleared. He realized at once that Linda would have to notice what he was doing and help without being told anything: He prayed that her face would give nothing away; Arcane would be watching them both for any indications of change.

He had not given Arcane the most important notebook; that was still on the bench where Linda had been making notes—in plain sight, if one knew where to look. All of the most important discoveries were noted in that newest book.

With any luck, he might also be able to give Arcane the next-to-last "soup" Linda had cooked up, the one he'd shown Cable on the third microscope slide. *That* fluid was startling enough in its properties to keep Arcane's labs busy for some time before they realized something crucial was missing.

Bruno handed the stack of notebooks to Arcane, who glanced at their spines. They were out of order, but plainly numbered. He rearranged them—numbers one through fourteen—and, satisfied, handed the stack back to Bruno.

Linda had a plan, too; but it did not mesh with Alec's. As he turned to take down the wrong container of solution, Linda suddenly rammed her elbow into Bruno's ribs and grabbed the notebooks from him. He lunged to grab her, but Arcane kicked Bruno aside and fired at Linda.

"Linda!" Alec breathed as she fell forward from the blow of the bullet and went sprawling toward the open door. The books splayed from her like a hand of cards.

Alec forgot the container and ran to her side. He lifted her limp head and felt for pulse in her neck. There was none. He looked away, his vision blurring with angry tears, and saw Cable's body lying outside in the foyer.

Bruno, like a child picking up toys, retrieved the notebooks.

"Take me seriously from now on," Arcane said. "Please, Alec." There was a note of regret in his voice, along with chords of menace.

Everything was lost. Alec got shakily to his feet, his hands wet with Linda's blood, and walked to the specimen racks. He abandoned his idea of deceiving Arcane with the wrong sample. He took the right one, the one that glowed fluorescent yellow as if it contained a piece of the sun, and walked toward Arcane with it. Alec remembered the explosions and the fires from even tiny droplets.

He walked past Arcane toward the door. He hoped to hurl it to the floor and burn the lab, and everyone in it, to the ground.

"Don't let him leave, Bruno," Arcane said, misinterpreting Alec's actions.

Bruno blundered into Alec with a body block that jolted him and sloshed the fluid over Alec's body. Instantly, Alec was a blinding explosion of green fire that enveloped him utterly.

He screamed. The men staggered back from the intense heat and light. Alec fell to his knees but rose again, flailing the air like a blind man, screaming. The flame was so bright that his body could not be seen; all that was visible was a pulsing globe of green brilliance. Alec ran through the door.

His sensations were more horrifying than painful, but

61

he knew that he was burning, that he was in shock, that he had to reach the water or become a pile of dead green cinders.

Arcane, Ferret and their men, racing after him out of the church, saw a vaguely human form inside an aura of light—a light so bright that the whole camp was visible, and long shadows turned like spokes as he ran.

Grasses flared into flame as Alec ran over them, and where he grabbed the railing of the wooden bridge a fire started. He dived into the water of the inlet.

He hit the water. Steam erupted in a boiling cloud, and there were repeated flashes and explosions under the water. Glowing clots of moss were tossed up into the air, and an eerie green vapor rose and seeped over the banks, almost obscuring the smoldering bridge.

Arcane looked back at the church, just as a low explosion rumbled forth from it and a whoosh of fire flashed briefly out the open doors. He spotted Bruno nearby.

"The notebooks!" Arcane spat out.

"I got 'em," Bruno said, holding the stack out for inspection.

"Good. Let's get out of here."

Two of Arcane's men had already carried a boat from its hiding place and were trotting it downstream from where the inlet still boiled and flashed. As Arcane turned to follow the boat, he instructed Ferret: "Stay here. Get rid of the bodies. Make sure there are no witnesses. Stay clear of the lab for a while; the chemicals in there are going to give you some fireworks."

Ferret handed Arcane a walkie-talkie. "Right. Your plane's ready to take off. Just radio 'em to tell them where to pick you up. When we're done we'll drive the jeep out —the long way around."

There was another explosion in the church, and the sound of splintering glass. They all glanced toward it; a billow of black smoke, fire-lighted from below, puffed up through the fragmentary roof of the old building.

Had that explosion occurred even a second earlier, Cable

62

would not have escaped. They would have seen her.

She was conscious when Alec's flaming body seared past her, though she was confused and not yet able to piece events together. By the time Arcane and his men rushed past, she knew enough to play dead; and when she saw that the lab had caught fire, she realized somebody might still be inside.

She scrambled to her feet and stumbled over Linda's body. She called out "Alec!" but in all the confusion was not heard by the men outside, who were spellbound by the fireworks erupting from the swamp.

All she saw of any significance in the lab was that notebook, the one she had seen Linda writing in, the one with the secret that had the power to change the world. She grabbed it.

A rack of chemicals near the security door was in flames. A large container exploded and sent a long finger of fire out the front door as it sprayed burning jets of liquid inside. Flames rose from lines on the floor and from one of the bookshelves where some of the burning chemical had splashed. Another chemical by the door sizzled into flame and sputtered up waves of black smoke. There was only one way out, and it seemed impassable, surrounded by fire.

But there was no option. The notebook in her hand, Cable shielded her face with her arms and charged through the flaming doorway.

Miraculously, the fire had not caught outside the lab, though there were little curls of smoke emerging from pinholes in the partition wall. She had the presence of mind not to bolt directly out the door, but first to look and listen.

Ferret and his men were standing in a semicircle near the old bridge—which for some reason was on fire—and they watched a spectacular chemical blaze that created dazzling fireworks in the swamp. Two other men were struggling with one of the little blue outboard boats. No one was looking her way.

Just as she rounded the far corner of the church, there

was an explosion inside; its concussion shattered the glass ceiling of the lab.

As Cable, her head throbbing, made her way deeper into the thick underbrush of the swamp, the old church exploded with a rainbow of colored fires. She tripped in the utter darkness and fell to her knees. Her hands hit the ground, and something slithered from beneath one of them. She began to cry like a little girl afraid of the dark; but that was the least of her sorrows. It seemed sure that she alone had survived whatever holocaust had taken place. And the deadly creatures of the swamp were minor threats compared to the unscrupulous venom of men.

9

A ground fog rolled in that smelled of rot and smoke and blew away before the sun rose. For a few minutes, the underside of a blanket of low clouds was blood red from horizon to horizon, then faded to gray as if the wrong morning was dawning and nature had decided to correct the mistake. After brightening, the sky darkened again; after warming, the breeze turned cold. A mist started to fall.

The creatures of the swamp were quiet. A bird called occasionally; locusts chirped now and again.

From where she sat, against a knobby, tangled cypress trunk, Cable could hear and vaguely see what was going on both at the camp and in the lake. Both sites were ghoulish. Bruno was picking through the ruins of the church, several others were wheeling the last of the bodies, weighted with stones, across the peninsula to dump them in the swamp. She had seen them bury nine. Now they carried the bodies of Charlie Tanner and Sam Darkow—the two, she dimly believed, who had died on the path in view of the infrared camera. Charlie. Nice, almost-honest Charlie—what had he been doing out there?

She heard a twig snap and realized that it might mean she would be found, but she scarcely cared. Her eyes were open, unblinking, fascinated in an unreal way by the impossible funeral procession. She could hear Ferret's grating cloying voice, but she paid no attention to the words. Her mind was in neutral—accepting data but not daring to evaluate it. She knew she was in emotional shock and tried to observe her state dispassionately. She suspected she breathed only about once a minute, and she had ceased being aware of her heartbeat. With very little effort she could convince herself that she was not there at all.

Another twig broke. Nearer.

She shrank farther into the roots of the tree.

A mud-crusted boot stopped not far from her hand.

Her heart began to pound again. She looked up, but the man's face was hidden by a low branch of the tree. The tree shuddered a little when he shoved against it, leaning.

The man muttered, "Goddamn sons of bitches," and she could tell that he was crying.

If he doesn't stop, I'll start crying again too, she thought.

Finding another person in distress roused Cable's brain. "Get down, out of sight!" she whispered hoarsely. "Now! Quick!"

He sank slowly and sat next to her in the crook of the crazy treetrunk. It was Bill Darkow. He said nothing, though he probably remembered who she was.

"We're the only ones left," she told him. "They killed all the others. Not just your brother."

"The Hollands?" he asked, his voice a gurgling whisper.

"Yes," she said. "And Charlie—"

"I saw them take Charlie . . . with Sam."

They sat without speaking, till he started to sob silently, and she rested a hand comfortingly on his knee. "If you get out of here alive," she said, "and I don't, you've got to get a report to Washington."

He nodded. "You can tell me," he said. "I'll remember. Damn right I'll remember."

"Washington's in area 206. You want JL5-2000. Extension 1919. Identify yourself as number 517. God, you can't remember all that."

"I think I can," he insisted. He smiled and wiped his cheeks.

"Ask to speak to your immediate superior. They'll connect you with a government security official with jurisdiction over this operation, someone in the vicinity. Tell them what happened, and tell them the man to nail is called Ferret, whom I think is working with someone called Arcane. They'll tell you Arcane's dead. I don't think so; Ferret's working for somebody. Show them where the . . . where the bodies have been dumped."

He nodded. "What are you going to do?"

"Get out of here the best way I can and try to deliver the same message."

"It'll be safer if we go separately," he suggested.

"Right. Tell me those numbers."

"Area 206; JL5-2000, 1919, 517."

"Amazing. I couldn't do that."

They watched Sam Darkow's body being slid into the muddy water. The murderers seemed mystically far away, pastelled by the mist; it made the splash sound unnaturally loud.

Darkow laid his hand over Cable's. "Thank you," he said humbly. "I'll go first. I'll head back along the west side of the peninsula till I reach the farm roads. Good luck, Ms. Cable."

"'Luck, Bill. And be careful, damn it. You walked right up here in plain sight. Keep *down*!"

"Uh, I have a better idea what's going on now. I'll be careful. You, too."

She smiled. When he had crawled out of sight into the sawgrass and cattails, she thought to herself in amazement: *What do you know—I can smile.*

The next thought that crossed her newly awakened mind was of the notebook. It was inside her blouse. Suddenly she remembered what it was and how it got there. She wondered whether she should have sent it with Bill, and decided that she had at least as good a chance with it as he would have.

A man's voice near the still-smoking church said something that contained the words "careful" and "hot"; and Cable wanted to hear more and to see what they were doing. Cautiously she moved closer.

The back of the church had been reduced to rubble, and tall marsh shrubs hid her passage to the very back of the

67

ruin. Bruno was in there talking to one of Ferret's mercenaries.

"Ferret says we don't get out of here till we find that
missing guard—Darkow."

"I thought they found his boat," said the mercenary.

"Yeah, but he wasn't in it," Bruno grumbled.

"What're you looking for? It's dangerous in here!"

"Bodies," said Bruno. "Just making sure."

The mercenary stepped high over black shapes that
smoked and occasionally flared into flame as he headed
out of the ruin. "Nobody made it through this," he said.

"Guess not," said Bruno, who continued to poke and
kick aside charred timbers and furnishings.

Another man wandered by. Chains and things were
dangling from his hands. He said, "I vote we get back and
have breakfast. All the bodies are at the bottom of the
swamp, and besides, I got all I can carry."

Bruno looked pensive and somehow affected by the
tragedy. Half-heartedly he asked, "What you got there?"

The man grinned. "I found some money, rings,
watches, a couple of—"

"No," said Bruno, "*that*." He reached out and took
the chain which dangled below the rest of the man's loot.
The chain was gold, with a trinket attached.

"Oh, that," the man said with a shrug. "Took it off the
lady scientist." He looked at Bruno and seemed to see
something dangerous in the big man's childish face. "You
want it? You can have it, Bruno. Ain't worth nothing
compared to the watches. One of these has a real computer—"

"Yeah, I want it," said Bruno.

"Okay," said the man, who was shorter by a foot and
lighter by a hundred pounds. He turned nonchalantly and
made his way out of the church. As he left, he said back
over his shoulder. "Wasn't that something the way Alec
Holland burned himself to a crisp? Damndest thing I ever
saw!"

Cable recalled a dim memory of a light flashing by, and
heat, and a man's tortured scream. She drew in a quick

sobbing breath.

Bruno heard her.

She ducked as he looked down the length of the remains of the lab to the smoking rubble of the back wall.

A timber from above fell and shattered into a cloud of soot, sparks and a tongue of fire. Bruno looked up to make sure there would be no more surprises and then made his way to the back wall.

Cable drew back to the nearest cypress trunk and slid behind it. She was well hidden but no more than ten feet from Bruno when he peered out. She heard Bruno cock his pistol. She found that she could see him, or fragments of him, through a tight clump of leaves at the base of the tree. He grabbed the hot rubble as he bent out to look around, and blew on his hands when he leaned back in again. "Ferret!" he called. There was no answer.

Cable slipped the notebook out of her blouse and stashed it in a deep cleft in the treetrunk.

As Bruno ambled back the way he had come—shoving aside hot timbers as if they were toothpicks—he held up the chain and opened the locket on it.

Cable leaned against the tree with a silent sigh of relief.

Next moment, Ferret yanked her to her feet with an awful laughing shout: "Gotcha!" His long bony fingers dug into the flesh of her arms as he dragged her toward where the bodies had been weighted and sunk.

She saw Bruno staring sadly, sympathetically, and she called to him, "Help me, Goddamn it!"

The big brute turned his head away.

"He's sentimental as a grandmother," Ferret chuckled; "but down deep he's a realist."

Three men came running up from the water's edge, where one of the blue boats was tied to a cypress, to give Ferret a hand. They rushed Cable to the boat and threw her in bodily. Two got in and held her down while the lanky, gray Ferret jumped in and instantly started the engine.

Alec had driven this boat last time she had ridden in it; Bill Darkow had driven it on her first ride. Ferret gassed the boat fast into the lake.

Bruno stood on the path, watching from the shore.

"There's a wonderful channel right about here, Cable," said Ferret. "Full of catfish, they tell me, and other kinds of scavengers. Water rats. It's like a river running along the bottom of a lake. Crayfish. Mosquito larvae. Alec Holland, they tell me, probably loves it down there. Water moccasins. Alligators."

Ferret flipped the motor suddenly into neutral. The boat coasted to a stop.

Without another word, Ferret pulled Cable off the floor of the boat and tossed her overboard.

She swam up to the surface, choking and struggling, and Ferret spread his spidery hand over her head and shoved it back under with a growl that was more an expression of pleasure than of anger.

There was a surge of bubbles, but she did not resurface. A moment later she came up with a gasp on the other side of the boat.

Ferret shouted with delight. The game was on! She began to swim away. Instead of pursuing her with the boat, Ferret took an oar and reached out with it, pushing her down again, slapping the water beside her head.

She came back up and lunged for the oar. He swatted at her with it again, and this time she gripped it and yanked it from his hands. He almost toppled into the water.

"Bravo!" he croaked. "Touché!"

The mist was turning to rain under a darkening sky. There was a rumble of distant thunder.

Cable flung the oar as far as she could and struck out for shore.

One of the men reached for the motor controls.

"No!" Ferret whooped. "Row, man! You have one oar left! Are you going to let her make it to shore? Row, man, row!"

The man tried to maneuver the wide motorboat as one would a canoe; it zigzagged as it chased Cable.

Her strength was waning; the boat caught up with her. With a shout, Ferret shoved her under again. This time he held tight to her hair. He felt her hands clawing at his wrist under water, but she did not come up. Bubbles burst around his arm. After a stillness, more bubbles broke the surface. Then nothing.

Ferret felt her hands relax and fall away from his wrist. He released her hair.

With a frantic struggle she surfaced again gasping, coughing. Her eyes were wide and her arms struggled aimlessly.

Ferret smiled. He took the remaining oar and, with great ease, pushed her down again. Bubbles burst. She sank as he pushed gently on the oar. Out of his perverse sense of order, he pushed all the way down until his hands were in the water. Rain drops made myriad circles on the still water.

Suddenly something huge and green and powerful reared out of the lake and seized Ferret's arm. A giant hand! It pulled him headlong into the water.

In the next second a gigantic shape loomed up with such a startling burst of energy that the boat flipped on end and sent its crew sailing through the air. They yelled as they splashed into the lake.

10

The boat floated upside down. The lake was quiet except for the sound of Ferret and his men treading water and raindrops striking its surface.

Then Bruno yelled from the shore, "Feeerrreeett!

And the men all looked and saw the same thing. Mountainous heap of a creature—glistening with slime, draped with rotting weeds, roughly the shape of a giant man—rose out of the swamp carrying the limp body of Cable. It kicked through hard cypress roots, snapping them like twigs, and lumbered onto muddy land.

"Don't just stand there!" Ferret yelled at Bruno. "Shoot it! Kill it! And kill *her!*"

The men in the water swam to the boat and righted it. They heard shots from Bruno's gun. When they looked again, Bruno was firing into the thicket at the shore, but the creature was not in sight. Other men ran to Bruno and followed him into the brush. Their pistols and rifles exploded like a chain of Chinese firecrackers.

"Ten to one," Ferret said to one of his men, "they're shooting at bushes."

Ferret was right. The men had immediately lost sight of the thing that blended so perfectly with the colors and shapes of the swamp. They were firing at where they thought it might have gone.

The gunshots ceased. Their last echoes blended with a thunderclap, and then the swamp was unnaturally silent. There was only the hiss of falling rain.

Ferret reached the shore and joined Bruno and the others who had backed out of the thicket, their guns still drawn but not knowing how to proceed. Ferret shook himself like a wet dog and snarled: "Go in there. Circle the area. The girl must not escape!"

The men were not quick to follow orders. Bruno said it for all of them: "What *was* that?"

Ferret said, in the manner of a sarcastic kindergarten teacher, "We'll never find out standing here guessing, will we?"

"Maybe the girl's already dead, drowned," said one of the men who came ashore with Ferret.

Ferret repeated, in precisely the same voice, like a stuck record: "We'll never find out standing here guessing, will we?"

The men reloaded their disarray of firearms and thrashed forward through the tangle of bushes, vines and dripping Spanish moss.

Deeper in the thicket, Cable lay hidden in a patch of marsh grass. Its sharp blades were tall and as thick as snakes. She coughed and spit muddy water from her mouth. Still struggling for awareness, she felt someone gently move wet hair off her face; and she thought she heard massive footsteps.

A burst of gunshots wakened her completely. She looked around and saw no one. She coughed again and tried to stifle the sound. She heard Ferret's rasping voice: "How can a thing that big hide? It's got to be here!" And instinctively she drew in around herself to make herself smaller. She heard rustle of bushes as the men passed; she saw no one.

But something moved low in the marsh grass nearby. Her eyes widened, and her skin crawled as if covered with gnats. A large alligator was ambling, lumbering from side to side, toward her. The blades of the tall grass bowed and snapped under its reptilian feet. Her face flushed; she hoped it would not react adversely to the scent of human fear. She remembered Alec's indignation, his defense of the alligator in the accident that she thought had killed her predecessor: "Well, the guy stepped right on the gator's head!"

Right now, she thought confidently, Alec would not be

73

afraid. Heaven knows what he *would* do, but he wouldn't panic or try to harm the gator. The thought calmed her a bit.

The gator came very close before it noticed her at all. It stopped and regarded her expressionlessly, except for a twitch of its wide-set eyes.

Its mouth opened, and Cable felt fear in every nerve end. A guttural gurgle emerged from between its spike-like teeth, and then the mouth closed. It had yawned. Bored with whatever the sight of Cable meant to it, it waddled off toward the water.

Cable came close to laughing aloud. She began to wonder how she had gotten here, how she had escaped from Ferret.

Ferret. She listened, tuned her ear acutely to distant sounds, and did not hear her pursuer.

Though water had stopped falling, it still sounded as if it were raining. Leaves and blades of grass crackled as they shed the weight of moisture and sprang back into place.

Cable pushed herself onto her elbows. Every muscle felt strained; she was extremely weak. Just as well, she thought, for she doubted that it was safe yet for her to stand up.

The majority of Ferret's men had trudged in the mire farther inland, but one had fallen back, had taken a different path. His name was Willie, and he prided himself on being as stealthy as a Seminole in the wilds of the swamp. He had always longed to catch birds with his bare hands, but he wasn't quite that good. The others hurried. Willie took his time. The others blundered through the bush. Willie climbed a short way up a tree and studied what he saw around him.

The sky was still completely overcast, but it was brighter now that the rain had passed . . . bright enough to make him curious about the smudge of blue he saw among the greens and browns. There was not much blue on the ground of the swamp—scattered violets and vibrant flecks of blue in a few species of birds—nothing like this smudge

74

of manufactured color that looked very like the gray-blue jacket Cable had been wearing.

Willie knew that if the quarry had indeed been found, the others were too far away to take the credit away from him. He was in no hurry. He wondered if she was alive.

He was watching when the alligator looked her over, and also when she raised up on her elbows. Then he saw her head of wet brown hair and knew he had her.

He climbed down from the tree and quietly—muffling the clicks with his hand—pulled back the pins of his shotgun.

His feet did not break a single twig, nor did he lower a foot flat enough to make a squishing sound in the wet moss.

He got close enough for his weapon to be totally effective and sighted her along the double-barrel—which he braced in the fork of a tree.

He mouthed, silently, "So long, baby."

Before he could pull the trigger, Willie heard a deep wheezing sound, like the breath of some titanic beast, coming from directly behind him. A huge forearm—wet, moss-green, large as a leg, with vines like blood vessels snaked tight around it—came down in front of Willie's eyes and pressed into his throat. Willie's last scream was strangled. His neck snapped. The gun he dropped struck the ground and fired both barrels.

Cable's heart raced at the sound of the close gunshots. She whirled in the direction of the sound but saw nothing.

Ferret's voice boomed out from the opposite direction:

"Willie? Did you get her?"

Footsteps and the tearing of underbrush came from the direction of Ferret's voice—toward Cable. They would surely see her!

She crawled, imitating the alligator, pulling her body flat along the ground, toward the muddy slush the gator had slid into. The reeds were taller and thicker there. She passed a cluster of green-brown orchid blossoms whose stems were tangled in, at one with, the dead stump of a tree—and she thought of Alec. The orchid he picked . . . what it grew into . . . splendid . . . how tragic that Alec had died in flames.

The alligator was there, lying still in inch-deep water. Mustn't step on its head, she thought inanely, on the verge of hysteria as she realized that death came at her from so many directions that she was safest lying here with a sleeping alligator.

She heard crushing sounds; something of great weight was moving slowly through the swamp. And she heard what sounded like the rumbling breath of a giant. She lay still, wanting the alligator to shield her.

Ferret gathered his men in a semblance of a clearing. "Willie?" he called again, this time more softly.

Ferret also heard the breathing and footfalls of a giant. They dwindled and stopped.

"Willie?" No answer. Ferret told his men: "Spread out."

Two men—the two who had been with him in the boat —flanked Ferret with their weapons ready. They moved into the thicket away from the clearing.

"Wait," Ferret whispered. "Listen."

They heard only the sounds made by the other men who were clumsily slashing through the underbrush.

"Such talent," Ferret muttered derisively. His two men caught his meaning and laughed, but nervously.

Something moved up ahead.

Without investigating, one of the two panicked and opened fire. His automatic blasted five times.

A man screamed, and there were shouts.

"Cease firing, you imbecile!" Ferret ordered.

Two of Ferret's men had been shot. One was dead. The survivor sat on the ground clutching his arm, whining, cursing. "Who did this?!" he demanded to know.

Ferret's eyes pointed out the guilty party—who stared down, speechless, holding a smoking gun. "You can kill him, for all I care," Ferret told the wounded man.

"Later."

Others had arrived. Ferret told them: "Bury this body with all the others."

The wounded man got to his feet, pulling himself up with the help of a bending branch. Ferret asked him: "Can you walk?"

If the wounded man had said no, he might have ended up among the bodies at the bottom of the lake. "Sure," he said.

Ferret nodded. "They'll take care of you at the estate. Beat it. Wait for us at the pickup point." He told the others, "Spread out; we're not finished here."

A minute later, a man yelled, "Hey! Here's Willie's gun . . . and —" Suddenly he screamed; his shout became a gag, and then there was a crashing sound in the bush.

Ferret's men were frozen.

"Come on, for Christ's sake," Ferret grumbled; "there are three of us. Just don't shoot each other this time."

Bruno took the lead and echoed his leader's accusation, "Yeah, don't shoot each other." They started out. Then Bruno stopped suddenly and bent down.

He had found two bodies—Willie's and the other man's. Their necks had been crushed and were bent back as if no bones remained in the upper spine.

Something bestial roared not far away, and from the same direction branches rustled and snapped.

Bruno said, "Ferret . . . don't you think maybe we should—"

"I think we should get the hell out of here," Ferret agreed. No discussion was required; the men raced, scrambled and stumbled back the way they had come.

Cable had heard shots and shouts and movement in the swamp that seemed to be getting farther and farther away. She lay on her back beside the sleeping alligator and gathered strength as she watched the clouds above thin and patches of blue appear.

The alligator grunted and waddled away, apparently unaware that it had had company.

The swamp sounded empty of humanity.

Even this far away, smoke still soiled the air from last night's fire; but the animals did not seem to mind. A fawn stooped to drink from the rainwater that had collected. Subtly as Cable moved when she sat up, she still startled the deer and it bolted away.

If a deer could drink that water, it ought to be safe, Cable thought. She cupped her hands and drank, then wiped the mud from her face.

She tried her legs. They worked again, none too rigidly, but they worked. She made her way around to the east of the peninsula. She saw where the helicopter had set her down in a sea of water lilies, where Bill Darkow had docked their boat. She remembered seeing the steeple of the church rising over the trees. It wasn't there now; a thin column of smoke rose in its place. She heard motors starting; they sounded like automobiles. If they were cars, where were the roads?

Staying out of sight as much as possible, she waded and swam across the inlet that served as a boat channel for the camp. As well as she could determine, no one saw her.

She pulled herself up onto mossy land. As she did so, a dozen water moccasins just ahead of her slithered into the water she had just vacated. She nearly fainted with horror. Her unwanted imagination gave her an image of thousands that had been coiling around her legs as she swam. After a moment she pulled herself together and went on.

Inland, she came upon two overgrown ruts that once had been a road of sorts; this she followed until it reached a flatter road more recently traveled.

She stopped for a minute to rest and heard—from somewhere behind her—a sound that belonged in an African jungle, something inhuman and more powerful than any swamp animal's. A deep, angry, agonized growl. She cut her rest short and ran down the newly found path.

11

The headquarters of the man who called himself Arcane was not far from the unsettled expanse of swampland in which Holland's camp had been located—not far as the helicopter flies. Even while impersonating Ritter, the camp's organizer and security chief, Arcane had been able to spend time at the estate that was his home, laboratory and retreat.

The estate—an antebellum plantation with modern structures grafted on—was self-sufficient, independent of any community, distant from any traveled highway, and never stumbled upon by accident. The civil documents that had once revealed its existence had long ago been purchased for a good sum, and had been destroyed. Deliveries for the estate—which included unusual furnishings and sophisticated scientific instruments and components —were made to a warehouse in Georgia, from which they were trucked by Arcane's own staff and vehicles.

The estate was, except to Arcane's associates, unknown. Yet many a monument with less to show has charged tourists for visits. The forty-seven rooms in the old main house were furnished with treasures that could fill a museum; the gardens were in competition with those of palaces, and contained dozens of species no botanist could identify; and the laboratory . . . . But the public would never be allowed to visit the laboratory or the rooms beneath it.

For all its opulence, the estate had no unifying theme, no essence. Anything and everything, provided it was valuable and/or one of a kind, could be given a niche there.

Once, Ferret had dined with him and joined Arcane in extravagant wine-tasting. Intoxicated, more candid than usual, Arcane had told Ferret: "The estate holds more than one man's taste, don't you see, because each of my moods has the potency of an average man. I have universal tastes and that means, of course, my good Ferret, that I have none. Preferences become trivial, don't they, when one's paramount goals are as boundless as mine? The estate is everything because I am everything. It's a mess, actually, valued at, oh, roughly two hundred million."

He sometimes called the place Arcane, as if he and it were interchangeable.

Holding companies, dummy corporations, foreign bank accounts, smuggling, stolen patents, government corruption and murder made it all possible. A large staff nourished it, and a small army protected it. He paid his people well and housed them on the estate; they gave him loyalty and surrendered for him any hope of winning prizes from the outside world. In this, he was not much different from many a leviathan corporation with its cradle-to-grave benefits and stringent rules of conduct.

These rules of conduct, even in light of the generous pay and the benefits, would never have appealed to Dr. Alec Holland, Arcane—a student of human behavior—knew. He had never bothered making Holland an offer. Instead, he had spent most of two years maneuvering Holland into a position of importance in Washington while convincing Holland that several of the Arcane dummy corporations had serious interest in the humanitarian implications of his work in recombinant DNA.

"I'm not proud," Arcane once told an acquaintance in Washington; "I know it when I see a brain superior to my own in a special field. In Holland's case, the brain is not for sale, so I must tap it on the sly." He added, "legally, of course."

Masquerading as Ritter, Arcane had watched Holland's progress keenly. He had known precisely when to send in Ferret's men—when to close down the operation—before Holland could reveal his discoveries or the government

81

could grow curious about its investment.

All in all, Arcane had thought to himself as his helicopter approached the estate the night before, it had worked out rather better than expected—if what he saw in Holland's lab meant what he suspected it did. He had carried the notebooks in his lap as others might protectively hold the mystic testaments of a new religion, or a newborn child.

He had carried them directly to his combination study and laboratory where he had begun with book one. It was a struggle to make out the family shorthand in which Alec and Linda had communicated; by dawn, however, he had been managing fairly well.

He called for a tranquilizer at seven; he was inordinately excited.

At eight, Caramel brought him his breakfast.

"The rain's stopped," she said softly, easing the door shut behind her. She stood just inside waiting for him to finish his thought and invite her in.

Caramel Kane. Senator Michael Kane's missing daughter, was twenty-four. She was an efficient secretary, an excellent listener, and one of the very few humans who could enter Arcane's study without being summoned. She was also quite beautiful, though she wore too much makeup to suit Arcane; he particularly hated the blue streak she insisted on maintaining in her otherwise splendid blonde hair. But he loved her for wearing glasses —as he loved anything that symbolized intellectuality.

Though the sky outside was brightening, Arcane's mineshaft of a laboratory remained gloomy. He alone sat in a pool of artificial brilliance—the result of several concealed spotlights aimed at his workplace from the two-story-high vaulted ceiling. Slatted wooden shutters were closed over the tall Tudor windows—admitting only slivers of hazy sunlight. The large room's walls were irregular, some flat, some curved; some angles were right and some not. Those surfaces not decorated with bookshelves were covered with wildlife trophies—heads of peculiar creatures mounted on mahogany. There were matching heads of something that looked to be a cross between a rodent and a wild boar; tusked, snouted, whiskered; a moose with antlers that were gnarled and unnatural; a gray lion and an albino bull; snarling dogs; horses; and hideous men: a child with two heads, aborigines laced like shrunken heads but, if anything, larger than normal, an ancient woman whose white hair hung down ten feet like some decorative tapestry.

The vines that snaked toward the ceiling spotlights were of a new dark green, leafy variety that could survive with little light and less attention.

When Arcane set his notebook down, stretched and turned to smile at Caramel, it was for her as if the shutters had suddenly swung open. "Is it morning?" he asked with a sigh. "Is that coffee I smell?"

"Yes, sir," she said beaming; "yes to both. Coffee with cinnamon and chicory, the way you like it, and grapefruit juice, dry toast, and crayfish with mayonnaise."

"Did you bring something for yourself? I'd like to have you join me."

She said coyly, "There's an extra coffee cup." She set the jingling silver tray ever so carefully on his black-topped work table.

The apparatus and variety of instruments and vessels on the table strongly resembled those Alec Holland had been working with—down to a duplicate of his special electron microscope. When Caramel lighted a Bunsen burner to slip under the carafe of coffee, the faint light was reflected along hundreds of glass tubes, coils and appliances. When she ran water from the cold tap of the lab sink into glasses of ice she had brought, the rattling and ringing echoed in the high-ceilinged chamber.

"You really should get some sleep," Caramel said with concern and devotion.

"It does the soul good to work through the night now and again," he said. "Elevates one's self-esteem, one's feeling of power. Don't you think so?"

"I imagine it would," she said.

He chuckled. "Do you know how honest you are,

Caramel darling?''

"To a fault?" she hazarded.

"Probably, though I find it refreshing—and unusual."
He sipped the coffee she had just poured. "Let's have a
little music."

She smiled and rustled softly over to a tape player on
one of the bookshelves. She selected a cassette and began a
program of Viennese waltzes.

"You would be absolutely fascinated with Holland's
work," Arcane said.

She returned and sat beside him. "I wonder if I'd
understand it?"

"In the broadest sense, the whole world will understand
it. His work with recombinant DNA is not so new anymore, but his combining of plant and animal cells is revolutionary—more even than he realized. It's astonishing.
Simple. And so beautiful."

"I'm glad you like it," she said, watching him peel and
dip a crayfish into the egg-cup of mayonnaise. "I mean,
I'm happy to see you pleased."

"Pleased," he repeated with a laugh. "I was close to his
discoveries in my own studies, Caramel, but I lacked the
spark he found to ignite it all. Genius, even in the hands
of a fool like Holland, is power. He'd have let it slip
through his fingers."

"But in your hands, sir, how overpowering! How magnificent it will be."

He nodded. He ran his fingers over the distinguished
gray at his temples and then down, with a regretful frown,
over his unshaven cheek. "I must look disheveled," he
muttered.

She snuggled close as if to say she loved him for it.

He rested a hand on her thigh, just under the edge of
her light-lavender spring dress. "How magnificent it will
be," he repeated, dreamily. He held a crayfish by the tail
and let it dangle halfway to his mouth.

Caramel waited patiently for him to come back to her.

"Lovely not to sleep," he said, "knowing that soon I'll
develop Holland's substance with my own hands. This

afternoon I'll give you a list of test specimens I'll need—animals, plants. I think we will eliminate the overcautious microbe stage Holland experimented with and go directly to . . . higher forms of life."

His coffee was half gone; Caramel filled his cup to the brim for him.

"It's exciting," she whispered, awed. "I want to be with you every step of the way."

"You see where it's taking us?"

"To the top of the world," she said with idealistic certainty. "The world will come to you—or starve."

He squeezed her leg. "I suspect that's largely true."

While he ate, Caramel picked up notebook number fourteen and strained to make some sense of it out.

"What's photosynthetic combustion?" she asked. "Sounds like a new engine."

"Let's see that," he said, taking the notebook from her. "These are the final notes; I haven't read them yet." He frowned at the page, then his mouth dropped and his eyes danced.

"It *is* an engine, my darling. A new engine for the essence of life!" He laughed in amazement. "Don't you see? Plants inhale carbon dioxide and exhale oxygen; animals do the reverse. But in a cell comprised of elements both plant and animal—nothing is lost! The efficiency of it staggers the imagination! The strength of it! The regenerative power!"

She gasped.

"You see it? You see it? No, I suspect not; you see only that *I* see it. Isn't that so? That was an empathetic gasp, *n'est-ce pas?*"

"Nest what? No sir, I'm sure that, compared to you, I don't see anything at all. But . . . but I had a thought. A frightening—"

"What is it, my child?" he said, rubbing her leg indulgently.

"Uh, if all the plants become like this, what will the animals breathe?"

Arcane was surprised by the question; he sagged against

85

the springy back of his lab stool. "For heaven's sake," he said, "my dear, you've made a *deduction!* But carry it further. See the reverse. Flip the coin. What new sort of animal will be *immune* to a diminishing oxygen supply? God! The idea excites me so I'll require another tranquilizer to see me through the morning. Will you see to it, darling?"

"Yes sir, of course. More coffee?"

"A wee bit, yes."

The soft waltzes playing in the background were interrupted by a melodious bell from the estate's intercom.

Caramel jumped to her feet, ran to the console by the tape deck and switched on the squawk box.

"Sir, Marsha's on her way to you with an important message," said a woman's voice.

"Thank you," Caramel said.

At that moment there was a hasty knock at the door, and Marsha—a dark-haired young woman with a lusty voice—hurried in.

"Sir," she began breathlessly, "I've come from the communications center—"

"One moment, Marsha," Arcane interrupted curtly. Something in notebook fourteen had caught his attention, something he seemed not to like. He closed it slowly. "What is it?" he asked the messenger distractedly.

"Ferret has just radioed, sir."

"Yes?"

"Something's happened."

"What?"

"He wants to speak to you personally, sir."

Arcane nodded. "Very well. Call him back and patch him through to me here." She turned to do as he asked. He stopped her. "Marsha, my dear, why don't you wear glasses?"

"Glasses? But, well, I have perfect vision."

"But not much of an imagination, evidently. That's all, Marsha. Thank you."

The door clicked shut behind the beautiful brunette.

Caramel set the intercom for a two-way patch to the

radio and returned to Arcane. She rubbed his shoulders, his upper back. "Something you read disturbed you, sir," she said. "What was it?"

Arcane relaxed into her soothing ministrations. "It could be a disaster," he said languidly. "I don't want even to think about it!"

"Oh, I'm so terribly sorry," she purred. "What is it?"

"The final entry in book fourteen is dated almost two weeks ago. Are we to assume Alec and Linda Holland were too busy making discoveries to keep notes? Not from their past behavior; no, we can't conclude that. Linda was overly conscientious about note-taking—some of these books are positively tedious—and Alec was not blessed with eidetic memory. No. It means that another book exists—or existed. The final book, the most important one."

"Perhaps that's what Ferret is calling to tell you. Perhaps he found it."

He moaned with pleasure and leaned his head back into her breasts. "You're why I surround myself with optimists, Caramel darling."

Ferret's voice, harsh and clipped, echoed from the intercom. "We've had some trouble, Arcane," he began.

"Who was left to give you trouble?" the great man said, diving to the heart of the question.

"Uh, we don't know. I'd prefer not to discuss this over the airwaves, Arcane—even though we're scrambled and rescrambled. I'm mainly calling to tell you that Bruno and I will need transportation back to the estate."

"You had a jeep."

"Uh, when we reached it . . . it was half buried in a quicksand bog."

"Who did that?"

"We don't know."

"How many of you need transport?"

After a pause, Ferret said, "Two."

After a longer pause, Arcane repeated the word. "Two?"

The gaps grew longer — as if interstellar distance imposed time lags. Ferret said, "Travis was wounded. I suspect he bought it in his way to the pickup point. Sperry was right behind us for a while, but . . . something got him.''

Ferret downed his entire cup of coffee. ''The others?''

''Dead.''

Ferret's eye landed on notebook number fourteen. ''Did you, by chance, find yet another notebook in the rubble? We've decided—that's the royal 'we'—that there has to be a fifteenth.''

''No, we didn't,'' said Ferret. His tone was slightly incredulous; he failed to understand why Arcane had turned to such an unimportant topic.

''Where are you and your muscleman?'' Arcane asked.

''The highway. The usual spot.''

Arcane sighed and got to his feet. ''I hope you brought a picnic lunch. You'll have a bit of a wait. I simply must shave and shower before I set foot out of here.'' He unbuttoned the top of his black silk shirt; Caramel took over and unbuttoned the rest.

Ferret said, ''Whenever. We have no place to go and no way to get there.''

''Over and out,'' Arcane said.

12

The shattered ribbon of concrete Ferret referred to was a "highway" only by comparison to gravel and ruts and ditches. Once a major bridge across solid land areas surrounded by swamp, the road had been replaced a dozen years ago by three lanes of asphalt farther north, which was not much of an improvement technologically but did better serve the huts and hovels and tiny towns of the few traditional swamp dwellers. The northern road connected to *bona fide* highways that carried one to civilization.

Mainly hidden by trees and hanging moss, the old road could be spotted from the air in separated places. It looked like a narrow, healing scar—which it was: grass pushed up through it and chipped away its edges, reclaiming the land for the swamp. Had an aircraft been flying over that day, an observer up there might have seen the only two vehicles on the road. Two fast-moving black dots. The observers would have missed the two pedestrians waiting at roadside, however; they were too thoroughly concealed by the trees.

One of the two pedestrians spoke. "I wish we *had* brought a picnic. I'm starving."

Ferret said nothing to console his big friend.

Then they heard it again. A wild, thunderous, animal cry from the swamp behind them. A wounded elephant combined with a hurricane. Another loud cry from not five feet away sent Bruno to his feet, wheeling his gun around: that had been an egret—probably as startled as the humans by the mysterious roar—which had taken to the air with a whooping cry.

"Jesus," Bruno muttered as he lowered his gun.

"Why didn't you shoot it?" Ferret taunted. "You could have eaten it."

They heard the approaching vehicles before they saw them. They stood at roadside waiting.

The lead vehicle. Arcane's black 1951 Cadillac limousine, belonged in a museum rather than a rutted road. It slowed to a stop. The jeep full of armed guards screeched to a halt behind it.

The guards, except for the driver, vaulted to the ground and aimed pistols at Ferret and Bruno. Ferret ignored them; he knew that their practice was only the result of excellent training. Bruno quickly pocketed his own firearm and briefly raised his hands as a measure of reassurance.

The two waited beside the limousine. They peered down at their own foreshortened reflections in the mirrored glass of the rear window.

The window hummed, and their images were replaced by the shaded face of Arcane, who was not smiling.

"You won't believe what happened," Ferret predicted.

"Try me," Arcane said. He did not open the door to invite them in.

"I want you to just wait here a few minutes," Ferret said. "I want you to hear it."

"Hear what?"

Ferret nibbled on his lip. "I don't know."

"Start at the beginning," Arcane urged politely. "Together, we'll make something rational of it." But still he forced the two to hunch over uncomfortably and report to him from outside the limo.

Ferret began with activities that commenced immediately upon Arcane's departure. He struggled for words to describe accurately what had happened—or seemed to happen—as he tried to drown Cable.

"One of the swamp people, obviously," Arcane said.

"I don't think so. I—I don't think he was human."

"Well," Arcane said condescendingly, "you go on with your story. You caught the girl again, I assume."

"Willie did. Or almost did. The thing got him first, broke his neck."

"The thing, you say. The *same* thing. You saw it kill Willie?"

"More or less."

"Which—more, or less?"

"Did you see him?" Ferret asked Bruno.

"Not that time," the big man admitted. "But I saw it good when it carried Cable out of the water."

"It—or *him?*" Arcane asked Bruno, his eyes challenging hypnotically.

"Him. Bigger than me, covered with . . . with green stuff."

"Naturally. He'd been swimming under water."

"Naked."

Arcane smiled a crooked smile. "That's eccentric."

Ferret insisted: "It killed the men."

"*All* of them?"

Ferret remembered the two who were shot by their own trigger-happy comrade but saw no point in diluting the point of his story with details. "All of them," he said.

Arcane looked from one to the other of the faces of the two who stooped low, as if bowing to a king, to report to him. "I'm listening, Ferret," he said.

Ferret looked at him quizzically.

"The beast of the swamps. I haven't heard it. Have you?"

"Not since you drove up."

Arcane nodded, frowning, wondering why Ferret and Bruno might lie about such bizarre encounters. "Ah," he said smoothly, "what of the girl? Was she dead when the swamp thing carried her out of the water?"

"We . . . aren't sure," Ferret admitted. "She may have been, but I had the impression that Willie was about to shoot her when he was killed."

"Yes, and why shoot a drowned lady? Right. Right." Arcane nodded slowly. "Did any of Holland's men survive? Don't say yes, Ferret."

After a long wait and an expression of chagrin that crawled over his gray chiseled face, Ferret said, "It's not likely, but possible that one of them may have. Bill Darkow."

Arcane nodded slowly again. As Ritter, he had known

the Darkow brothers rather well. "Brave lad. God-fearing no doubt. Obliged to risk his neck to see that justice is done. Uninformed, though. He probably understands little of what went on back there."

Arcane opened the rear limo door and said, "Get in."

Now Ferret and Bruno were not quite sure they wanted to. Arcane had interpreted their valiant tragedy as a failure.

"Might as well," Arcane advised them. "Or don't you think we've listened to the swamp long enough?"

Ferret shrugged. He held the door for Bruno to enter first.

"Listen!" Bruno whispered, half in, half out.

A rumble, it might have been a trick of the mind, came from the swamp.

Arcane shook his head.

It came again, stronger, although its source seemed farther away than it had the time before—as if the thing were retreating farther into the swamp.

The third time, even Arcane identified the sound as something wild and unusual. He said, as Ferret and Bruno settled into the limo's jump seats, "On the radio you said Travis was wounded. Should we send someone in after him?"

Ferret thought over the possibilities—including that he himself might be sent back in—and said, "I wouldn't bother."

"You know best," Arcane said.

The limo made a laborious U-turn—it was longer than the road was wide—and started back toward the estate. The jeep followed.

"The girl you lost," said Arcane, "who may be alive, is a greater danger to us than Darkow. She is what she claims to be, right enough, but because of her sensitive work and security clearances the lady also answers to the FBI at home and the CIA abroad." He smiled and settled back into the plush camel-hair seat. "You grasp the problem, I'm sure. We—that is, *you*—will go back for an air search."

13

Along the dirt road, Cable passed by the remains of three shacks: their porches were piles of rotting planks: windows were shattered; walls leaned and were obscured by cudweed and rampant honeysuckle. The wheelless remains of an old Ford rusted in what once must have been a driveway. Three neighbors, long gone.

But the road had to lead somewhere, and there was evidence—tracks and broken weeds—that the road was sometimes used.

She heard a radio playing country music before she turned a bend and spotted a solitary shack with a couple of gas pumps and an old telephone booth.

The sun was out now, and the ground steamed. It had been more comfortable in the rain.

Cable trudged up to the phone booth and folded open the screaming green-metal doors. The phone was covered with rust and dust. She lifted the receiver and listened. There seemed to be something there—like the sound a seashell makes held to the ear. A yellow sticker on it called for a dime. She rummaged in her pocket; miraculously, she had a dime. She tried it. Still she heard only the sea in the seashell.

There was a boy leaning back in a straight chair propped against the porch wall. He was watching her, but with little interest. He was in shadow, and his skin was so black all Cable could see were his eyes. He idly waved a fly-swatter back and forth until he realized Cable was watching him. He let the swatter fall into his lap.

She approached him. "Hi," she said.

His eyes scanned her up and down. Closer now, she

guessed he was no more than thirteen.

He said, "You been in a plane wreck?"

She laughed. "No, I—just out for a walk."

"Uh huh."

Cable imagined herself as he saw her: trousers still damp and caked with mud, torn in places, her blouse and jacket in no better shape. She suspected she had twigs and seaweed in her hair and knew there was soot on her arms and hands. She laughed again. She found the kid instantly likeable.

"Got a phone that works?" she asked.

"Inside," he said. He let his chair down with a clunk and held the screen door open for her.

The room just inside was a gas station prepared for one customer every day or two. There were a few cans of oil on a sagging shelf, a dispenser of fifty-cent road maps, and miscellaneous auto parts scattered around. A little plastic radio rattled with a static-plagued station.

With the boy's help, she reached a country operator who reluctantly agreed to process her collect call to Washington. She listened with growing desperation to a series of electronic switchovers and finally a ringing buzz.

"Two thousand," said a woman at the other end. She agreed to accept a collect call from Miss 517.

There were more clicks and electronic atmospheres, and finally a man said, "Operations. Clark."

"This is 517," she said, "Cable."

"One moment." He put her on hold, presumably to call up her identification and files on his video display.

"Go ahead, Cable," he said after a moment.

"Operation Marshland," she said. "Please connect me with my nearest contact. And hurry. I'll hold on. This is quite urgent."

"Have you a report to make?"

"I'd rather make it in person to my local superior."

"Hold again, Cable. I'll see what I can do. The man you want is Colonel Ritter. I'll locate him for you."

"No, wait—" she tried to stop him, but he had placed her on hold again. Ritter, she felt sure, had been killed.

95

Someone else would have to be found.

The black boy was watching her wide-eyed, intelligently. Nothing about his face moved except his eyes.

"We've got Ritter for you," Operations said at last. "I'm going to patch you through."

"Oh, thank goodness!" said Cable. "Listen, if a boy named Bill Darkow contacts you, help him all you can. Put him in touch with Ritter."

"Says here Bill and Sam Darkow were on Ritter's staff."

"Right, but the men have been . . . separated."

"Here's Ritter for you. Is there a number where you can be reached?"

She gave him the number on the dial of the gas-station phone, and after several clicks and a buzz found herself awaiting a new party.

The boy said to Cable, "There's been some killin', hasn't there?"

She looked away from him.

Only a few miles away, Arcane, in his car, had taken the Washington call. Patched in Washington, it had been patched again by Marsha back at the estate; and now the call was returned to the swamp from which it originated.

Learning from Operations that an operative named Cable wanted to reach him, Arcane's voice became suddenly deeper and more abrupt, less cultured, less pleasant. Even his posture adapted to the slovenly shape he had used as Ritter.

"Yeah," he said to Operations, "put the call through."

"Ritter?" Cable's voice sounded half a planet away.

"Where the hell are ya, Cable? You calling from the compound?" Arcane had his driver flip a switch that amplified her voice over a conference-call speaker for the benefit of Ferret and Bruno.

"Where the hell were *you* last night?" she asked angrily. "The camp was attacked. You don't know?"

"No. What happened? Who attacked?"

"Christ, I can't go through all that again now. I'll tell

96

you later. Everything was wiped out. The Hollands were killed. I thought *you* were dead.''

''Shit. I took a night off. Where are you?''

''Uh—just a minute.'' She was evidently asking someone for help with directions. She came back on to say, ''At a gas station about a mile south of the road to the lab. On old farm road 87.''

Arcane's driver slammed on the brakes and began to maneuver the big limo into another U-turn. The jeep following close behind had to run off the road to avoid a collision.

The cursing guardsmen jumped out to help push the vehicle out of the muck and back onto the road. Bruno laughed.

''I'm not far from there,'' said Ritter/Arcane. ''What did you tell Washington?''

''Nothing much. I said I wanted to report to you— except I didn't know it would be you.''

''You sound upset. Calm down and wait for us. Rest. Uh, Cable, did you . . . manage to save anything?''

Arcane held his breath waiting for her reply.

She said, ''Damn right. I've got the last notebook.''

Arcane's face was suddenly transformed. He almost slipped into his own persona. He cleared his throat to re-engineer Ritter's voice. ''Good work. That's something anyway. Sit tight. I'll be there before you know it.''

''Thanks.''

Arcane tossed the phone handset back into the front seat. When the driver had switched it off, Arcane said with a giggle, ''Ah, if there's a god of the swamp, I should get on my knees to him tonight!''

Bruno said gravely, ''There may *be* a god of the swamp.''

Cable used the station's surprisingly clean restroom to get some of the mud off her skin and out of her hair. The windowscreen was alive with huge mosquitos that could not quite get in. A dragonfly landed on the screen; the mosquitoes merely rearranged themselves. Feeling refreshed, relieved that help was on the way, that the horrors of last night were over, she strolled back inside the station to wait.

Fishing for a quarter in her ruined pockets, she found a quarter and dropped it in the slot of an old red round-topped Coke machine. Nothing happened.

"Doesn't anything work around here?" she asked the boy—who had not taken his eyes off her.

"Just me," he said, deadpan.

Cable gave the machine a swift kick. The boy walked over to her, concerned for his property. He said, "Kickin' it don't help none. Just spoils the paint."

"Sorry."

"You got to punch it." He hauled off and rammed the machine with the heel of his hand. The thing rocked on its base, rattled and coughed an icy bottle down into its delivery trough.

Cable grinned. "Thanks."

"Nothin'. Name's Jude."

"Mine's Cable."

The boy stuck out his hand. Cable smiled and shook it.

Before they were introduced, the silence had not mattered; now Cable felt obliged to engage in small talk. She looked around the room. The place was wretched in the extreme—it had a desk and an easy chair—and the boy wore clean but old clothes. She almost meant it when she said, "Nice station."

He just blinked.

"Your dad own it?"

He seemed to be on the verge of saying something but changed his mind. He shrugged and looked away from her.

Cable sighed. Evidently the boy did not share her impulse for a chat.

A few minutes later, he said, "Looks like your ride's here." He was staring out the window past her.

Cable turned to hurry out the door and stopped short. Pulling up was a tall old limousine—shining like new, like something from a time machine—definitely not govern-

98

ment issue. It stopped at the phone booth. No one got out.

"Ever see that car before?" she asked Jude.

"Nope. I'd remember it, too." He stood beside her so they could both see out the front screen door. Cable was sure no one outside could see them, as it was much darker inside.

A jeep careened around the limo and pulled up to one of the tow gas pumps.

"They get their own gas," Jude said.

Cable knew what he meant; the jeep's gang of five were dressed for jungle warfare and armed to the teeth. She knew more; she knew these were dressed and armed like the men who had raided the camp.

"Some friends you got, lady," said the boy.

"They're not," she said, as much to herself as to Jude. "I wonder what they're doing here."

"You runnin' from 'em?"

"If they see me, I'm cooked."

"Uh huh," he said, not moving.

Ferret emerged from the limousine. He looked into the phone booth, checking the number or checking to see if it worked, and looked from the booth to the station. He carried his automatic rifle as casually as a grouse hunter stalking a treeline.

"Is there another house with a phone near here?" Cable asked Jude.

"Not with, or without."

As Ferret ambled toward the screen door, Cable and Jude backed away and ducked behind the desk.

"Don't be afraid, Jude," she said, her own heart racing.

"Say that to someone whose desk you ain't hidin' behind," he said in his level voice.

She looked around. There were screened-in windows on either side of the door Ferret approached and one other window on the side near the gas pumps—where the jeep was parked, where its occupants loitered.

"Is there some way out of here I don't know about?" she asked Jude.

"Yeah," he said, "through my room back there." He pointed with his thumb over his shoulder. "But it don't open to the back, just to the side. It goes through the bathroom."

"The side by the gas pumps, or the other side?"

"Other side."

Ferret was only a few feet from the screen door. He called out, "Anybody here? You open for business?"

Cable got ready to run; she had a sudden thought. "Is there a gun here, Jude?" she whispered.

"What kinda place you think this is?" he whispered back. " 'Course there is."

He opened the center desk drawer and reached up into it, fumbling until he brought down an ancient rusty revolver with oily receipts stuck to it.

Cable grabbed it.

Ferret opened the screen door.

"Stay here," she whispered to Jude.

"Took the words right out of my mouth," he mumbled back.

She half-crawled, half-lunged through the door behind the desk.

Thinking fast, Ferret ran back out the way he had come and circled the shack.

Cable was waiting for him. "Hey, you!" she yelled, "drop it!"

Ferret coolly ignored her and squeezed the trigger of his automatic.

Cable leapt into a pile of old tires. A storm of dust and tire fragments rose from around her. Ferret's firing pin fell on an empty chamber.

Cable rose up and fired at him point blank. The old gun gave off a terrific explosion, fire kicking out the side of the rusted cylinder; then the gun literally fell apart in her hands.

"Oh, great," she moaned, hurling the gun aside, and turned and ran down a path toward thickets and marshland.

Ferret slammed a fresh clip in his automatic and laughed. As the jeep rounded the corner of the station, he jumped in, still laughing, and urged them down the old pitted drive into the marsh after Cable. Bruno was driving.

Cable had made a mistake. The old road was solid; the quicksand on either side of it was not. She was a bowling pin at the end of a lengthening alley, and the jeep was rolling toward her.

But the jeep had a problem, too. The road was so full of deep holes that it could not gather speed. It lurched and bumped like a maddened beast hellbent on revenge, while the occupants held on for dear life. Only Ferret, standing front and center and holding the top of the windshield, seemed at ease on the bucking machine. Bruno's knuckles were white on the steering wheel.

"Faster!" Ferret commanded. "Run her down!" he yelled loudly enough for Cable to hear. She was about forty yards ahead; the distance between them was shortening perceptably.

The jeep hit a rock-hard rise in the road and one of the men in the back flew out with a scream. All four wheels left the ground.

"Faster!" Ferret commanded again. Twenty-five yards now. He stared only at Cable, thought only of her.

But Bruno saw something rising out of the swamp just beyond Cable. His foot eased back on the accelerator.

"What are you doing!?" Ferret demanded.

"Look!" Bruno shouted, his voice high and pinched. "It's back! It's that thing!"

"I don't care," Ferret snarled, refusing to look. "Run her down."

"We've got to stop the car!"

Ferret poked his gun barrel into Bruno's side.

"But it's that thing!" Bruno whined. Nevertheless he began to accelerate again, timidly.

Ferret jammed his left foot on top of Bruno's flooring the pedal. "I want her before *he* gets her!"

Bruno struggled with the steering wheel. "Where'd it go? I don't see it!" he said, scanning the way ahead frantically.

101

"Maybe you never saw it," Ferret growled. "Hit her! Hit her!"

Cable was only feet ahead, stumbling, only seconds from death.

Suddenly a huge, moss-encrusted, human-shaped monster burst up from the bog and planted itself squarely in front of the jeep.

"Don't stop!" Ferret screamed—crazed, obsessed, his foot still bearing down on Bruno's. "Ram it!"

The jeep rocketed ahead. The thing braced itself and shoved out its two massive arms.

The crash was grinding, grating, explosive. Ferret sailed over the monster's head as the windshield snapped forward; his automatic flew out into the quicksand.

Cable ran even faster to escape flying debris, men and weapons. The jeep's engine was thrust back into the firewall as the body wrapped around the creature's massive form.

The headlights sprang off like eyes popping from their sockets. Smoke and steam rose from the ruined hood and a hubcap continued ringing down the road; the jeep had been stopped dead as a bike hitting a linebacker.

The sound of the crash reverberated through the trees; it turned into the rustle of a gentle breeze.

For an eternity that was only a few seconds, nothing moved. The scene was like a frozen frame of film: the monster still braced, one giant foot back, one knee bent, against the jeep. The men still inside were too stunned to stir; those on the ground lay quiet.

14

Bruno peered up over the dashboard right into the thing's face. It had a face, a human face, but one malformed and exaggerated. A great primitive brow ridge hid amber deep-sunk eyes. A nose stripped to cartilage flowed into cheeks that looked hard as bone. A wide lipless mouth, a chiseled slit that seemed sculpted of unfinished granite, was part of a powerful square chin. Hairless, the skull was interwoven and made to bulge by tangles of tentacled roots. The face—the entire creature—was the earth-green color of muddy swamp vegetation.

Bruno stared at that face and body and quite literally held his breath.

Others recovered and also were spellbound by the thing's appearance. Its musculature—webbed and defined by what looked like roots but might have been external veins—was awesomely beyond the possibilities of human development. His skin had the unreflective texture of matted moss; but it was like felt covering shapes of iron.

The thing seemed unaware that a dozen eyes were appraising it. It was preoccupied. Its huge eyes wide, it was looking from the destroyed vehicle to its own massive hands, and from the hands down to its monumental naked body. It seemed to be surprised, alarmed, by its own strength, by realities it had not imagined.

Slowly it removed its hands from the jeep and stood erect. It was easily over seven feet tall; and from the way it tipped its head to turn its attention to the mere mortals down in the jeep, it had not previously realized its outstanding stature.

Had Arcane been there, he might have been the one

bright enough, shrewd enough, with enough presence of mind, to observe that the creature was at that moment undergoing an awakening of intelligence, a maturing of self-awareness. But his men were too dumbstruck to entertain such notions.

Cable felt something, though, in the form of an overpowering fascination and the conviction that whatever it was, it *knew* what it had done. She wondered if it knew *why*.

As if the creature read her mind, it turned and looked for her, spotted her where she crouched by the side of the road. It gave her a direct fiery look of strange, frightening intensity.

She shrank back, terrified.

One of the gunmen cautiously climbed out of the wrinkled jeep. He hit the road, dropping his rifle, and ran back toward the gas station. Another, who sat on the ground shaking sense back into his head, saw the defector and thought he had a good idea; he got shakily to his feet but stumbled again to his knees.

With a rumbling shriek of rage, the monster thundered to the side of the jeep and ripped off Bruno's door as if it had been paper. The door sailed out and splashed in the mire.

"No!" Bruno yelled as one of the enormous green hands reached toward him. "No, no!!" He reared back and fell over the awakening body in the other front seat.

The thing grabbed Bruno's arm at the shoulder and wrapped sinewy fingers completely around his ham-like biceps. With leverage that might have broken the man's arm, the monster hoisted Bruno into the air and with its other hand thrust against his rear to sail him into the swamp like a model airplane.

Bruno screamed like a man falling from a building till he plummeted into the muck and came up flailing, battling weeds and water lilies to reach firm land.

Ferret's ears were still ringing from his tumble, but he was wide awake and his mind was in gear. He established that the aching pains he felt did not indicate broken bones, got slowly to his feet so as not to attract the thing's attention, and walked casually to the automatic rifle the defector had dropped in his flight. Ferret aimed from the hip and opened fire.

A continuous stream of high-power bullets exploded into the air and dug into the flesh of the swamp thing. The creature's mouth opened and a roar of rage emerged that competed with the booming gun. Bellowing mightily, the giant stumbled backward, jolted by the bullets that tore at his flesh and sent green fragments flying. Another gunman opened fire from the back of the jeep.

Incredibly, once the monster recovered somewhat, he was more enraged than injured. He turned on Ferret while the man's bullets were still digging into his body and, his arms menacingly wide, advanced into the gunfire.

Ferret stood his ground, his automatic pumping, until the last bullet was used. Then he dropped the weapon and snarled, intent upon suicidal combat with this super-human killer. Ferret's bony gray face seemed more than ever like a grinning skeleton's, and the profound hatred radiating from his eyes would have terrified most men into submission, hypnotized them as a cobra does its victims.

But Ferret's evil only enraged the monster. It would have torn him in two—if Cable had not screamed.

The creature wheeled. One of the gunmen was holding Cable against him as a shield.

"Get back!!" the gunman screamed shrilly, without a shred of confidence in his voice, "Or I'll kill her!" He fired the last of his bullets into the swamp thing's chest and then, dragging Cable with him, he backed toward the jeep. Beyond the jeep lay safety; beyond which—sil-houetted against light at the start of the tunnel of trees —stood Arcane and his driver, watching.

Frozen by fear, the gunman released his grip on Cable. The monster lifted the man high into the air and slammed him, shattering his spine, onto the rocky road. It nudged the body into the quicksand with an enormous green foot

and watched it settle down out of sight.

When the creature looked around again, he seemed to be alone.

The jeep still steamed and hissed; everything had taken place in a minute, though it had seemed like an hour.

The creature leaned against the jeep, breathing labored, deep and halting; it was weak and in pain; its huge head sank onto its chest. The metal of the jeep creaked, bending under its weight.

There was a sound, a rustle of leaves.

The thing lifted its head and listened, straightened its back and sniffed, taking in great volumes of air.

A bush at the roadside moved.

The monster charged toward it with a violent growl. He swiped down and tore the bush out by its roots.

Cable—who had been hiding behind it—screamed.

She felt dizzied by the terror that gripped her and clouded her eyesight.

But the monster stopped. It made no move toward her. It stood straight and, startled and curious, cocked his head to one side.

She sprang to her feet and ran.

It took a few tentative steps toward her but stopped again.

Cable waded out into the swamp, away from the road. She backed away, watching the creature who stood still as a tree and watched her through interested amber eyes.

She stopped. Something like sap was oozing from the ragged bullet wounds of the creature.

Cable realized she was sinking. She had waded into quicksand. She panicked at first and fought the mud to get out. The movement sank her deeper. She could feel that the deeper she sank the thicker the substance under there became.

The creature made no move to hurt her or to help. He continued to stand there watching with interest, breathing slowly and audibly.

She collected her wits; she was, at the moment, more afraid of the swamp than the creature. She had sunk almost to her shoulders. She remembered what she had been told about quicksand: struggling makes you sink; you must swim or pull yourself out with your arms. She did something against all instinct; she leaned forward, sinking more into the mire at an angle, and stretched out her arms. An easy breaststroke pulled her forward, and she felt her feet rising, coming out of the thicker goo.

The green monster just stood and watched.

She had no choice but to swim roughly toward him: that was where vines grew that she could use to pull herself out. The cool silt infiltrated every fold of her clothing until she felt naked. Twigs and clots of dirt suspended in the thick liquid scraped her body as she pulled herself along. Before she reached the bank she was lying face-down on the surface, breathing to one side.

When she stood dripping at the edge of the road, brown silt streaking her body from head to foot, she wiped her eyes and found herself not ten feet from the monster who stared at her as before.

There was a hefty stick near her foot; she picked it up and held it ready.

The creature turned and, as if it had learned all it wanted to know, shambled off slowly into the trees.

When it was out of sight she heard its splashes for a moment. And then the swamp was quiet except for a whine of insects.

Cable dropped the stick and backed away from where the creature had disappeared. Her heart was returning to some kind of normal beat.

Something touched her back, and she spun around. It was the wide-eyed black boy from the gas station.

"Jude! What are you doing here?"

"You think I'm gonna stay around that station with everybody pumpin' it fulla holes, you mistaken," he said.

"Did those men leave? The other car—that limousine?"

"They got in and drove away. Temporarily. Heard 'em say they's comin' back." As was his manner, Jude had been sizing her up with his X-ray eyes. He shook his head.

"Can't manage to stay clean, can you?" He shot a glance at the crumpled jeep. "What happened to that thing?"

"Um, it hit a tree," Cable said.

"Uh huh. Must've been one of them hit-and-run kind of trees. Don't seem to be there now."

"No," she agreed, unwilling to elaborate.

The boy looked at the muddy ground. Near his bare foot was the clear imprint of a foot five times as large. Most of his foot fit into the thing's big toe mark.

Jude said, "Some tree, alright." He stared off in the direction Cable had been looking. The long shadows of late afternoon made the swamp especially spooky and dense. The boy turned to Cable. "There's this trapper's cabin I know. You can stay there till morning. Swamp's no place to be at night."

"I know," she said, grateful for his thoughtfulness and unsure how he'd want her to express it.

"C'mon," he said, "I got a boat."

His boat was tied to an old dead cypress only a hundred yards or so farther along the bumpy road. Here a ridge of land held back the mire, and a shallow clear waterway—almost invisible beneath lilies and sawgrass—led deeper into the forest of moss-draped trees. Jude propelled and steered his flat metal skiff with a long pole he pushed against the bottom, working from the bow while his passenger rested on the wooden bench lashed across the stern.

He seemed to be concentrating on landmarks Cable could not find; she did not disturb him with talk.

The yellow rays of the sun came at a low angle, where they penetrated at all, and Cable noticed a haze forming through the trees. It obscured detail, emphasized distance. An alligator climbed out of the water onto a jut of land. It did not frighten her; she watched it with curiosity and interest.

She caught Jude's eye. He had seen it, too, and had regarded it much the same way. He said, "But I seen one take a man's leg off once for no reason 'cept maybe it was hungry."

"Thanks for the reassurance," she said sarcastically.

"Welcome," he muttered as he returned his attention to the path ahead.

The trapper's cabin had no lock on the warped front door. One window still had glass in it; the other three had been tightly boarded over. Not much light found its way inside. There was a smell of mildew and dust.

Jude took a kitchen match from a Mason jar and lighted a hurricane lamp. "Let's look around for spiders," he suggested. "I hab 'm been out here in a while."

There were two dusty cots, a broken rocking chair, several empty fruit crates, a porcelain-topped kitchen table with patched legs, and a wood-burning stove.

Jude said, "A skillet's in that box by the stove, and some cookin' things."

There was also a stack of dry wood.

"If there were anything to cook," said Cable, "I'd make you some dinner." She sat on one of the cots and reached down to pull off her wet muddy boots.

Jude stood at the open door, black anyway and now just a skinny silhouette with eyes and teeth. He scraped the door back and forth as he thought something over. "You start a fire?" he asked her.

"Sure."

He thought a minute more and said, "We got fish. And blueberries. I planted carrots in back—if they ain't rotted away by now. An' sassafrass tea, taste like root beer. If you really wants company."

"I really do," she said. "I'll start the fire. What do we do for water?"

"Drink the swamp. Bad some places, but around here there's springs. Ain't killed me yet."

Jude brought in half-a-dozen carp a few minutes later— they spawned in the shallows at sunset, and he grabbed what he wanted—and while Cable built the fire and began to dress the fish, he gathered a pan of fresh blueberries and collected the paltry survivors from his neglected carrot patch. The sassafras root he promised for tea had been collected in another season and was stored in jars stacked by the stove.

"Do you do everything by yourself?" she asked him. He was showing her a better way to scale the fish.

"Most times," he said.

"Live by yourself?"

"Anymore."

"Like it?"

"Okay."

Thin clouds gathered over the breathing swamp. They turned orange in the late sun and their color was reflected in the water of the swamp. The trees and shadows were lavender, gray and black.

Cable and Jude ate near the open door and watched the spectacle of the day petulantly relinquishing the swamp tonight.

"Can you make it back the way we came after the sun goes down?" Cable asked.

"C'mon!" he exclaimed, insulted.

"Well, do you want to? There are two cots."

He stopped a carrot halfway to his mouth. "Don't take me wrong, but . . . bein' aroun' you don't make me feel 'zactly safe."

"Suit yourself."

The swamp then made a deep sound, a mournful sound that could not have been the wind.

Jude said casually, "On th'other hand . . . ."

111

15

In a wild cypress grove, a conspiracy in nature grew a ring
of perfect trees, draped each with looping vines and a lace
of moss, and nurtured each from the deposits of a nitro-
gen-rich flowing stream.

Among the searching roots of the thriving trees, roots
that resembled human limbs, stately egrets and flamingos
waded in serene safety. A hundred species of orchid were
in riotous bloom.

The water encircled by the trees was clear, over a
smooth-pebbled bottom.

The uppermost leaves of the cypresses caught the red-
orange of the lowering sun; the water of the round pond
was orange with the image of clouds, and flecked with
black from the deep shadows of the coming night.

A bulky, lumbering shape waded into the pond. Syrupy
amber tears oozed from amber eyes; it was like the fluid
that bled from his numerous wounds. His mountainous
shoulders sagged; his head looked down at the rainbow of
washed pebbled under the orange and black surface. His
tears blurred the image already fragmented by the rippling
water.

When he reached the center of the ring of trees he
stopped.

He looked up.

The red disc of the sun sat on the trees of the horizon
which were a dimensionless cut-out, a light gray silhouette
torn from the paper of twilight.

His legs were weak. He wanted to sit, perhaps to lie

under the water and become nourishment for the beautiful trees.

But the sun . . . he could not tear his eyes from it; it would not let him move. Faint as was its power at sunset, he could feel its life-bringing heat on his face, his arms, his body.

While he stood thus transfixed, transported, the symphony of creatures preparing for nightfall began to interrupt its songs. The bullfrogs stopped and the treefrogs subsided; one last bird *caaawwwwed* long and loud as it flew away carrying its cry with it; a large animal splashed into the water somewhere and then the water calmed again; cicadas signaled a time of vespers to one another, and the last of them—somewhere in the distance—ended its grating whistle.

It was absolutely quiet.

The swamp thing looked at its ungainly hands, its pain-torn arms, its inhuman body, and bellowed into the silence. The sound came not from a throat or a mouth but from an entire being, from deep within him. It was a broadcast of agony such as the world of man has never heard.

He stared again at the sun—as a man might search out the face of God, or a child his mother's eyes.

The sun, too, was silent.

It continued its relentless drop into the light-gray trees, its dimming, its betrayal. The red of human blood seemed a personal mockery.

The swamp thing cried out again. Root-like cords in his neck strained and vibrated. His hands became fists.

This time he was answered.

It was not the sun who answered.

It was the swamp.

The trees.

His sound came back to him—deeper, older, a million voices no man could hear. He looked around him. The water at his thighs rippled in the silence as he moved abruptly.

The last of the sun's red touched the trees, touched their

uplifted arms, rimmed their leaves and edged their roots. It was a marvel, a revelation!

Though only a fraction of the sun remained above the distant row of trees, still he could feel its heat; he was growing more and more aware of it, sensitive to it.

Its servant.

His eyes widened and his granite mouth opened in astonishment.

He looked at his arms. The bleeding had stopped. The sun was healing him.

Again came the sound of the trees, low, comforting; and he heard branches rustling in the breeze. But the air was deathly still.

The water rippled again as he turned to look at the trees all around him; their generous lower branches were waving.

A voice in his head said: "I think like a tree sometimes. I know how they feel about sunlight and wind and rain and chills. See these cypresses? They're the happiest trees in the world."

The largest cypress seemed to beckon to him. He took a sloshing step toward it, stopped and turned back to look at the sun.

He saw the sun now as a tree sees it. He nodded in tribute as the last rays winked into eclipse behind the horizontal row and sent up a wide hand of farewell.

The cicadas began to sing again.

The swamp thing waded to the big cypress and leaned against its ample trunk, one knee bent and a giant foot against the smooth wood. He crossed his arms—which no longer hurt him—and watched the sky. He watched the orange dry-brushed under the clouds retreat slowly from east to west, following its master.

Then he watched twilight lavender follow the orange and the clouds dim from gray to charcoal.

Stars appeared between drifting clouds.

He was aware of a pressure against his side.

The tree was trying to hold him.

He curled up among the roots, and slept.

16

The concealed ceiling spotlights singled out a plush conversation alcove in Arcane's laboratory and study. Ferret and Bruno lounged in semi-reclined cradles facing Arcane —who sat stiffly, alone, on a loveseat dating from more straight-laced times. They had come together for drinks after each had bathed, dressed and dined in their separate quarters.

"Some of the men say it's one of those abdominal snowmen come to the swamp," said Bruno.

"Interesting opinion," Arcane said with a derisive snort.

"I'll tell you, it was like hitting a tree," said Ferret. "And bullets hurt him, but they didn't stop him."

Caramel Kane wheeled a mirror-and-marble motorized bar into the soft circle of light. "The usuals, gentlemen?" she asked so rhetorically that she had begun to mix before the three didn't bother to answer.

"My goodness, Bruno," Caramel said, handing him his beer and vodka, "what happened to you? You're all bruised! You, too, Mr. Ferret!" Ferret got straight bourbon.

"Lovely lady," said Arcane smoothly, "we encountered a beast today, and as a matter of fact, the boys and I were just about to discuss what to do about it." He waited with his hand outstretched till she slipped the stem of his brandy snifter into it. "What would you do, Caramel darling, if there were a dragon residing between you and your heart's desire?"

She grinned. "Ask you to slay it for me."

Arcane chuckled. "I wonder if Ferret and his sidekick

115

here will be as rational."

Ferret shook his head; his long, gristled neck twisted like a turned rope. "I say we forget this damn notebook. It's not worth it. What are we killing ourselves for?"

Arcane laughed. "Eternal life," he answered.

"Seriously," Ferret pressed on, "all for the formula for some new plant fertilizer?"

"Ferret," Arcane said sadly, "you disappoint me. It's nothing so ordinary as that." He stood and strolled toward the outer edge of the pool of light. His trousers and shirt were black; Ferret and Bruno watched his floating head and gesturing arms. "Something extraordinary has come out of Holland's experiments—something I had no notion of. Gentlemen, would you recognize immortality if it knocked on your door?"

The two looked at him dumbly.

"Well, obviously you wouldn't. But that's beside the point." He put his hands behind his back. His head floated at the edge of darkness like a talking balloon. "I believe we have over- or underestimated Holland's potential—depending upon one's ethical point of view."

A strange dog with long toenails clicked across the floor and curled up with a plop at Arcane's feet. He stooped and lifted the creature into his arms. "Ah," said Arcane, "my little friend, Scruffy." He mussed the dog's long straight hair and set it down again. The fellow had front legs much shorter than his normal rear ones and a neck narrow as a broom handle. His head bobbed as he walked. "Poor chap will die before long," Arcane told his listeners. "His rib-cage is much too limited to permit development of adult heart and lungs. As if you, Bruno, had built-in limitations prohibiting your development past, say, the age of 15."

Bruno said, "I got an extra-big rib cage."

Arcane downed the last drop of brandy and handed Caramel his glass for a refill. "I wonder what your score will be tonight, Bruno. Will you miss *every* point I try to make?" He stepped back into the light and took Bruno's empty glass. "Here, let me have that freshened for you."

The intercom chime sounded.

Caramel switched it to loudspeaker.

"Arcane here," he said for the intercom's microphone.

The compressed voice said, "You have a guest, Mr. Arcane. A government agent named Bill Darkow."

"I've been expecting him," Arcane told the woman's lovely voice. "Send him to the laboratory."

"Very well, sir," said the voice.

"Hey!" said Bruno loudly, "you caught—!"

Arcane shut him up with a withering look. "Over and out," Arcane said amiably. The loudspeaker went off with a faint pop.

Ferret laughed at Bruno. "Arcane hasn't told the bastard what the set-up is; Darkow doesn't know he's caught."

"Quite so," said Arcane. "He called via Washington —just as Cable did. He allowed our driver to fetch him so he could make his report to Ritter. Remember Ritter?"

"How much does he know?" Ferret asked.

"Little or nothing, I should think," said Arcane. "He's just a loose end, one we mustn't leave dangling. There is a chance, however, a small one, that he'll know what happened to the final notebook."

"How important is he, aside from that?" Ferret asked.

"Not at all. Not to me, or you, or the world. Government agents are interchangeable. Like ball bearings. Ready for another, Ferret?"

"Wouldn't mind," he said, handing Caramel his glass. "Also wouldn't mind taking care of Darkow for you, when you're finished with him."

Arcane said, "Your games are going to get you killed, Ferret."

Ferret grinned a cadaver's grin. "Can't think of a better way to go."

"Oh?" Arcane let his eyes drift to the ceiling. "I can."

There was a knock at the door.

"Let him in, will you, Caramel?" Arcane asked. To Ferret and Bruno, he said, "To continue with my point, I suspect our friend Dr. Holland was more unscrupulous than we knew. I believe that swamp thing might be a crea-

117

ture of Holland's design—one of his failures."

"You said he only experimented with plants," Ferret said.

"That ambulatory green superman is no plant," said Arcane.

"What's ambulatory mean?" Bruno asked.

Arcane ignored the question. "That is to say, he's no plant in any ordinary sense. If I interpret Holland's work aptly, that monstrosity could well be immortal, its cells forever regenerative. Think . . . *think*! If I—or you, Ferret, or you, Bruno—could incorporate its kind of cells in our own bodies! Immortality!"

Bill Darkow had been brought in and stood by the bar observing Arcane and his two listeners, puzzled.

"Make our guest a drink," Arcane said. He did not offer a chair. "I want that swamp thing," he said to Ferret.

"Don't worry," Ferret said with narrowed eyes, "I'll blow him away for you."

"I want him *alive*," Arcane said.

Darkow pointed to the bottle of Scotch; Caramel poured and signaled for him to say "when." He made a "cut" swipe with his flat hand when the golden liquid had covered the ice.

"Excuse me," Darkow interjected during the lull, "I need to see Colonel Ritter. Is he—?"

Arcane affected his Ritter voice and posture and said, "There's been a drastic change in plans, Darkow. You'll get new instructions."

Bill looked pale; he said nothing.

Arcane ignored Darkow and continued talking to Ferret. "I want that thing alive. I want to study his living flesh. He carries in his veins pure elements of the formula that determined him."

"All right," Ferret said reluctantly. "How do we find it, and how do we catch it?"

Arcane wheeled on Darkow suddenly and demanded loudly, "Tell me about the fifteenth notebook!"

"What?" Darkow asked incredulously.

Arcane studied him acutely. "No, you don't know," he decided.

"Who *are* you?" Darkow asked.

Arcane waved aside the question with a flick of his wrist, as one might get rid of a fly. He had no more interest in Darkow—neither to inform him nor to confuse him.

"Is your name Ferret?" Darkow asked him.

"No," Arcane said. To Ferret, he said, "How do we catch it? I think that's just the sort of sporting proposition that would appeal to you. Think back. Every time you've seen Beauty, you've seen the Beast. Right?"

"Huh?" Bruno said, bewildered.

"Right," said Ferret thoughtfully.

The pathetic little dog sat at Darkow's feet, whimpering for attention. Darkow looked down at it in horror. He returned the drink he had barely sampled to the portable bar. It had occurred to him that he might need all his wits to leave this place alive.

Caramel noticed the rejected drink, misinterpreted it and asked Darkow in a whisper, "Would you rather have something to eat?"

He shook his head. His body was flushed with fear; his mind was on red-alert.

"All we have to do," said Arcane, "is catch Cable and keep her alive long enough to draw the monster out. Take Beauty; the Beast will follow." As an afterthought: "It doesn't exactly maintain a low profile."

"No," said Ferret, "but *she* does."

Arcane turned to Darkow and asked him, in a friendly voice, as if the government man were one of his associates, "I don't suppose you know where the lady would hide, do you, Darkow? You were one of the few out there who seemed to know your way around. You and your brother."

Darkow didn't answer.

Arcane answered for him. "No, you couldn't find her. She, after all, only arrived yesterday, and you hardly know her. Besides, *she* doesn't know where she is, as you would in her place. Hmmm."

"That means she could be anywhere," said Ferret.

119

"It means she's lost; but she's on foot and within a certain radius of that gas station."

Darkow, though a diligent student and dedicated soldier, was not equipped to deal with the situation he found himself in. His thoughts swirled in a solution of fear and confusion. The aristocratic hawk-faced man—how could he have Ritter's voice!? Was it murder these men were contemplating? Did they have the insane impression that Darkow would help them? Had they destroyed the camp and killed his brother? Probably—but why? Were they working for Washington? Did Cable get her call through? If so, why wasn't she caught, too? Who were they kidding about this monster of the swamp? Was this all just a game? Could it be a nightmare, unreal?

I've got to get out of here! Darkow thought suddenly. He jumped a little at the thought—as one jerks sometimes falling asleep—but immediately composed himself and resolved to take it easy, take it one step at a time.

There were high windows up under the vaulted ceiling, he saw, but no noticeable way to reach them. Unless—could one climb the bookcases? In the gloom up there, Bill could not at first see what the knobs and larger protrusions on the wall might be; then he realized that they were trophy heads. But what kinds of animals—?

He shook his attention back to the center of the problem. Even though these men were apparently paying no attention to him, he kept his movements to a minimum so as not to betray his inner workings. He took a single step back into greater shadow.

There were several doors and windows around the large room; he could see them through mounds of lab equipment and towers of glass tubing. It looked like the Hollands' lab. Was this guy working on the same—? He wrenched his curiosity away again.

He thought: If I *can* get out of here, if those doors lead to freedom, why are these nuts ignoring me?

"More drinks all around, Caramel," Arcane said, "then you may be excused."

"Not me," said Bruno; "I've had my limit."

"Yes, yes, you would be one of those people with limits," Arcane said absently. He switched to Ritter's voice and said gruffly to Darkow, "Hey man, you not drinkin'?" He picked up the scarcely touched Scotch. "Drink up. Puts hair on your chest."

Darkow said, "No, thanks. Are you going to let me go?"

Arcane ignored the question and said, back to his own voice again, "Now let's see, who was at the gate this evening? Alicia, wasn't it? Pretty brunette with a cruel mouth?"

Darkow nodded.

"Did she search you for weapons?"

Darkow licked his lips. He had no idea how to answer the question, so he told the truth. "She asked me to leave my pistol with her as a courtesy."

"And you did, of course. Fine. Fine. You must have imagined you were under the protective wing of the great American Eagle. Well—not exactly." He lifted Bill's drink from the bar and held it out to him. "Here, take this. I really insist."

Bill did as he was told.

Ferret rose to his feet and stepped toward Darkow. Bill's hands and feet tingled. The man was monstrous: grayish skin stretched tight over bones and stringy muscles, broad-shouldered, half a foot taller than Bill, his eyes smiling one kind of smile and his mouth another. His gold earring glinted in light from high above.

Bill felt that if he didn't drink from the ice-cold glass in his hand he would drop it. It seemed to make no difference which he did. He drank a deep draft and caught his breath as it burned down to his stomach.

Ferret said to him, "You're a healthy-looking boy. Do your calisthenics every morning?"

Bill nodded, his mouth open; terror and disorientation had hypnotized him.

"Before or after your shit, shower and shave?"

"Before."

Arcane took another brandy from Caramel and held the

121

bourbon she had poured for Ferret. He blew her a kiss—
which was her signal to go. She blew one back and started
the electric whine of the motor in the bar. She let it pull
her toward the door.

Ferret continued to interrogate his intended victim.
"I'll bet you do just about everything right, don't you,
Bill? Steady job with a moderate amount of excitement,
eight hours sleep a night? You married, Bill?"

"No, but—"

"Ah, there's a lady somewhere. Just one, I'll bet.
What's her name?"

"Gail."

Bill managed to shake himself out of his passive state.
The girl heading for the door was going to open it! He
tossed the Scotch in Ferret's face and ran toward Caramel.

He was too early. She had not opened the door yet—
though there was a key in her hand—and she had sense
enough to wait. Bill grabbed for the key; she tossed it to
Bruno.

"I'll let you out, sugar," Bruno volunteered. He climbed slowly out of his recliner, as though he was aching all
over, and walked like an old man to Caramel's side.

Bill had darted from his failure with the key to another
door—one that seemed to lead directly outside. It was
locked.

Ferret cut him off before he could reach the third door.

The last door was in a corner not far from the conversation alcove. It had a handle rather than a knob, and in
the split second before he opened it, Bill realized that no
one was bothering to stop him.

A fluorescent light flickered on in a long refrigeration
chamber. Strong odors of preservatives and decay assailed
him as Bill gaped into the metal tunnel. There were
animal and human corpses, in various stages of autopsy,
and shelves of limbs and containers of organs. There was a
row of human babies—misshapen, contorted—and something that looked as if it might have been Siamese triplets
all massed in a single hideous lump.

Arcane saw the subject of Darkow's horror and said

122

pleasantly, "Marsha had that one for me. Like it?"

Bill backed away as Arcane closed the heavy door. Bill backed away and stepped on the queer dog—which emitted a cork-in-a-bottle squeal. Its spindly neck had snapped. It was dead.

"Nothing you can do about it when your number comes up," Arcane mumbled as he picked up the little body. "Get it over with, Ferret."

Bill's heart sank as he heard the door a long room away click shut. The muscleman had helped Caramel leave with her bar, and now he guarded the door.

"Drive a new American-made car, I'll bet," Ferret said, "and you always will. Grow roses when you retire from government service?"

Darkow sprinted for one of the black lab tables. He grabbed a flask from a bracket and threw it at Ferret.

Ferret laughed. He spread his arms batlike and walked relentlessly toward Darkow, who continued to throw glass. Ferret said for the benefit of Bruno and Arcane: "Just like this afternoon when that other unstoppable monster walked into my gunfire. I know how he felt! Invincible!"

Bill threw a beaker of fluid. Ferret sidestepped it; it sizzled as it cracked and its contents ate into the hardwood floor.

Ferret kept coming and Darkow kept throwing—anything he found loose on the table. He hoped to make it to the end of the workbench and, from there, to the window. He'd throw himself through it . . . .

Suddenly he felt a pain in his back and a convulsion in his chest. He heard Arcane say:

"Sorry, Ferret, but this has gone on long enough. I can't have my lab in shambles."

Ferret asked: "What did you do?"

Arcane said: "Simple surgery."

Bill felt his knees give way as black splotches converged in his eyesight. Then everything went black forever.

Arcane was behind the collapsing body. He tossed a bloody Byzantine dagger into the lab sink.

Bruno walked over slowly and looked down at what was

Bill Darkow as if he had never seen a murdered man before.

Ferret regarded the body too, but with indifference. "Have any use for this?" he asked Arcane.

"Not that springs to mind." He laughed. "Too bad we haven't any pet alligators to feed it to. What are you staring at, Bruno?"

"Nothing," he said turning away.

"Why don't you trundle off to bed?" Arcane suggested. "You've had a busy day, little man."

"Don't call me that," he said quietly.

"A busy day, *big* man," Arcane corrected, making it worse, accusing him even more of childishness.

"Can I have a girl?" Bruno asked Arcane hopefully.

"Certainly, Bruno, almost any one you want. Marsha? Celia? Dawn?"

"Terry," said the big man.

Ferret guffawed. "No taste in women either. Old plain Terry."

"She—" Bruno began defensively and stopped short.

"Wild sex?" Ferret supposed.

"She likes me," Bruno got out with acute embarrassment.

"We'll see if she's available," Arcane said draping his arm over the top of Bruno's thick back and leading him to the door.

"Do I have to have a shot?"

"I think not, Bruno. No more experimenting for a while, till we have Holland's formula. I suggest you and Terry go so far as to take steps against pregnancy."

"Okay. 'Night, Mr. Arcane. Are we starting out early in the morning?" He stepped across the threshhold and waited obediently for instructions.

Arcane nodded. "Helicopter, I suspect. I'm not sure you'll be needed, Bruno. Check with me around seven o'clock."

"Right," he said. He pulled the door shut. " 'Night, Mr. Ferret," he said, just before the lock clicked. Ferret did not respond, and apparently Bruno had not expected him to.

Ferret asked Arcane, "What have you got against Bruno? He's one of the few I trust."

"Like I said earlier, he has limits. He may be reaching his limit for . . . doing whatever may be necessary. But if you want him tomorrow, take him." Their last drinks were on a lab table, untouched. Arcane took them and delivered Ferret's to him. "Exciting times, Ferret," he said, making a quasi-toast and half-raising his glass. "We're at the start of an enterprise you and I will never top. Inhuman sacrifices will be required of us."

Ferret mulled over the implications of that and asked, "Such as?"

"Who can say?" Arcane sipped. "The phrase 'survival of the fittest' may be about to take on a world of new meaning."

"What about tomorrow?"

"One day at a time, eh? An air search. You lead it while I arrange for the delivery of some new equipment."

Ferret nodded. He raised his glass. "To the future."

"All of it," Arcane agreed laughing.

17

The next morning was clear, and cooler than it had been. There was very little ground fog for the sun to dissipate when it finally rose.

Cable and Jude were out just ahead of the sun, in Jude's little skiff. The black boy poled them through a passage in the cypresses that was like a subterranean cavern. The floor was a carpet of blooming lilies that parted obligingly to let the boat pass and then closed solid again. The walls were broad treetrunks; above, admitting the sun only in spots like confetti, the canopy was a cathedral vault of branches and leaves.

Everything, the boat included, was dew-drenched and sparkling. Clouds of large blue dragonflies flew and hovered, darted and drank, low over the white blossoms among plate-sized leaves.

"He was right," Cable said to herself. "It is beautiful."

A bullfrog jumped from one lily pad to another.

"Who was right?" Jude asked.

Cable woke up in the here and now and sat straighter. "Guy I knew. He loved these swamps."

"He wasn't so crazy. Listen."

"To what?"

"Hear any danger?"

She shook her head.

"See? Only big mistake God made with the swamps is mosquitos."

"Good thing for me you know your way around," Cable said, smiling.

He nodded. "Reckon it is."

A large green leaf lighted on the hand Cable rested on

the boat rim. The leaf had legs. Cable saw Jude watching it without concern, and she held her hand still.

"That's a katydid," Jude told her. "Look so much like leaves the trees don't know better. Mantis looks like sticks. Butterflies look like flowers."

She nodded. Jude had become a bit more conversational since they first met.

He asked, "Can't you call that guy that loves the swamp? Maybe he'd come get you outa trouble."

Cable averted her eyes and shook her head.

He understood her silence. "Ain't nobody you can call?"

She cracked a wry smile. "Actually, I thought there was. But when I tried him, those goons back there showed up to make Swiss cheese out of your gas station."

He gave the pole a strained push and the boat skimmed a little faster. "They weren't glad to see you," he agreed. "You didn't pay your bookie or something?"

"Or something."

The tranquility of the morning was marred by a sound they both recognized. It came from the distance, got very loud, and then trailed away: a helicopter.

"Much farther?" Cable asked her boatman.

Jude surveyed her, saw a return of yesterday's apprehension, and shook his head. "Just a little ways."

She leaned over the edge and picked a huge white water lily.

Jude asked, "What you got to go back for? You said they totaled the place."

"I have to get something I left there."

"Somethin' more important than gettin' away from the goon squad?"

Cable nodded gravely.

Jude nodded with her, deadpan, mocking and at the same time conceding: if you say so. He poled toward the bright end of the cavern of trees, where it met the shallow lake around the peninsula of the ruined camp.

They were not alone in wanting to return to the camp that morning.

Ahead of them, already wading in the water of the inlet, the fearsome monster of the bogs and marshes returned to the pool that gave him birth.

As if the ruins emitted some kind of ray that became more harsh the closer one approached, the swamp thing fought off tensions and agonies that grew stronger with each sloshing step. He ripped away a hanging vine that was in his way, and the violence of it startled a snake heron which took to the air with a piercing cry.

There was an acrid odor of smoke in the air.

He looked for the steeple and saw nothing rising above the trees.

The bridge was still there. He stopped in the water and looked up at it. Where his blazing hand had touched the railing there was a charred area—and several sprouts, green shoots that grew with the grain and curved up looking for sunlight.

Lumbering up through the mud and tall grass, he swiped aside a dozen cattails, and trudged—amber tears forming in his eyes—toward the church. The wreckage of everything about it was devastating.

He shoved timbers away, and a black billow of ash blew into the air; he snatched up what was left of the old oak front door and sailed it like a stick, angrily, across the compound.

He made his way, first, to the arboretum that had been along the side wall. His tough bare feet shattered the remains of what had been the glass enclosure.

Moving among the shriveled corpses of a thousand plants, he paused to touch them tenderly as a father might his lost children.

He moved into what was left of the laboratory of Alec and Linda Holland.

He passed from one disaster to another—sooty meltdowns of exquisite instruments, shattered racks of beakers and vials, the gutted remains of the electron microscope. Cable's voice came to him: "You ought to put a cover on that." He dropped what was left of the circuit box into the ashes on the floor.

128

His tour of horror ended at the burned-out socket of the wall safe where the notebooks had been secured. There wasn't an ash that might have been one of them. Someone had them. He stared into the safe and, like a pilgrim at the last station of the cross, sagged at the emptiness.

He was too preoccupied to notice the sound of a pole scraping the metal bottom of a boat as it reached shore, or the low voices that were not made by breezes in the trees.

Jude and Cable dragged the skiff through the grasses and propped its prow on mossy land. They stood by the boat, ankle-deep in water.

Cable said, "You stay here, Jude."

"Don't worry," he said. "I planned to."

She took a step away and turned back to say, "If you see anyone coming, give a yell."

The boy gulped and nodded. "Don't worry."

Cable tried to sound casual but failed because she was frightened herself. "And if you yell and I don't come, then just go on and get yourself out."

Jude's eyes widened perceptibly. He said nervously, "I can handle myself. Don't worry."

Cable smiled reassuringly, impressed by the boy's courage. "I'm not worried," she said.

She climbed up the bank and headed directly around the side of the church toward the tree at the rear where she had hidden the notebook.

Cable missed hearing Jude mutter to himself, "Well, *I'm* worried."

Some of the studs of the side of the church and the lab's interior wall still stood, but there were tall slats of air where planking had been. The side looked rather like open venetian blinds turned sideways. She did not want to look in. The building was a corpse. There was something indecent about being near it, like an invasion of privacy. She kept her eyes on the charred path to the back.

She walked quietly—though she could not have said why. There was no sign of anyone else.

Suddenly her ear picked up something from inside the church. An animal, she told herself, or maybe rubble fall-

129

ing, burned splinters blowing.

She waited a moment, and then walked on.

She heard it again. Something was moving inside. Something, from the sound, picked up a piece of debris and tossed it aside.

Hiding behind a shrub, she peered inside. She saw nothing at first. Then something near the ground stirred. She saw a massive green back, the back of a huge head. Strangely, he was kneeling, and rocking back and forth. He was intent upon something at his knees on the ground. He reached down and scooped up something from the ashes. What, Cable could not see; his giant body obscured his hands.

He had picked up Linda's locket from where Bruno had sentimentally placed it: on Linda's ashes. Fumbling, his hands too large, he managed to trigger the spring. The locket opened. The face inside was that of Alec Holland— a handsome, square-jawed smiling man, with blue eyes and light brown hair and skin that was fair and modeled by a light reddish suntan.

His hideous face grim, driven, the moss-covered exaggeration of a man laid the locket where it had been. Then he wrested himself upright on his knees and shakily to his feet.

Cable continued to peer out from behind the shrub, hoping he would not hear her or look her way.

The creature pawed his way through a jumble of charred wreckage. He pulled out a rack of test tubes that had somehow escaped damage. Carefully, almost tenderly, he carried the rack to a half-burned table.

Cable wanted to see better. She stood and walked right up to the wall studs. She kept herself ready to run. What does it think it's doing? she wondered.

He returned to the wreckage where he had found the test tubes and tore into the rubble; he dug frantically. He lifted a large buckled cabinet and placed it on the ground gently. Inside he found bottles of chemicals that were still whole, and several graduated cylinders. He placed these with extraordinary care on the burned table.

Out of the pile he next pulled a rectangular shape, an instrument of some kind. He looked at it, rubbed it as Aladdin did his lamp, and then hurled it away. It crashed not five feet from where Cable stood.

She did not budge; he did not look her way.

Cable thought of chimps she had seen in shows, animals that mimicked the behavior and movements of humans with such precision that audiences implicitly believed that the animals had the same motives and knowledge as men. This ape of the swamps, this prehistoric humanoid was miming the actions of someone absolutely familiar with the laboratory and its furnishings. This *thing* had watched —who? Alec, Linda?—laying out implements for experimentation.

Even more incredibly, he picked up a vial and seemed to be holding it up to look at the contents. But the great beast was too clumsy, his hands too massive and powerful; the vial burst under the pressure of his grip. The monster reeled back, surprised. He let out a sharp snarl of anger.

Cable was terrified by her own compulsion to stay. She felt as she might if she were in a foreign land she had never visited before—seeing the face of a primitive native who looked hauntingly familiar to her. It was absurd.

With shaking, fierce concentration, the creature tried again, this time to decant the contents of a beaker into a test tube.

Cable watched the muscles of his enormous tendoned back and arms; his body was incredibly tense, active, attempting to master some kind of control. His legs stiffened.

But the fragile beaker slipped from his clumsy hands and smashed against the floor. The monster's lunging attempt to prevent this only heaped disaster onto accident, upsetting the entire rack. A horrible domino reaction began and glass containers toppled, rolled, fell and shattered.

The beast howled in frustration. He slammed and splintered the table with a single blow. Enraged by his own rage, he struck out senselessly to break the nearest thing he saw—a timber from a roof truss. Then he reeled through the charred mess, smashing everything within his reach—cabinets, shelves, bookcases, tables, materials.

Suddenly he stopped. He listened. He looked directly at the slot in the wall where Cable had been standing. There was no one there now.

Cable had fled. She had run directly toward the old tree —past the slotted half-destroyed wall, in easy view if the creature had happened to look or hear her running. But his violence and noise had kept him occupied.

She reached the tree, fumbled in its roots, found the notebook and frantically searched for a way back to Jude that would not take her right past the church in the open.

She picked out a path that seemed safe enough.

Once, when she was halfway there, she risked exposing herself to see if the monster was still where she had seen him last. The crashing sounds had stopped.

He was there, looking vaguely in her direction, but nothing indicated that he saw her.

Jude was in the boat, waiting. He had readied the boat for a getaway.

She jumped in.

"You took your time!" he said accusingly. Then he read a peculiar change in her face. "What happened?"

"Just go!" Cable said. She caught herself and lowered her voice. "We're just going to do our job and get this notebook back to Washington."

"Oh. Is that our job?"

"It is now." She grabbed the pole from him and gave a hard shove against the bank that sent the skiff splashing into the water of the inlet. As she gave another, harder shove, she said to herself, "The rest isn't my business!"

The skiff skimmed toward the water of the lake.

The creature stood in the doorway of the burned church watching her go. There was unmistakeable sadness on his monstrous face. His mouth opened slightly. A word tried to come out. It died as a rumble in his cavernous chest.

He turned to go in again. Something caught his eye over where the ladders to the living quarters on the balcony were still bolted in place. The dining table was there. So was the orchid.

While everything else that had been living had perished in the fire, the orchid that had burst out of its pot and sealed a bond with the table had not. The leaves and blossoms of the lower part had been destroyed, but a new shoot was now three times the height of the stem at the time of the fire. The upper portion was triumphant, virile green amid the black ashes, and it was in exquisite rambunctious bloom.

He lowered his head and buried his nose in the largest flower. His eyes closed for a long moment.

Suddenly he jerked upright. A sound . . . something out on the lake.

He ran to the bridge and looked down the inlet.

Out in the lake, cutting across the channel and the creature's line of sight, a loud and fast airboat passed. It was perhaps a quarter of a mile away. There were two armed men riding in it.

18

Its great caged propeller howling, Ferret's airboat plowed through sawgrass in shallow water at the speed of a racing auto. Ferret's loose-fitting commando khaki flapped in the gale like a hurricane flag. Bruno's boyish face was wide-eyed, excited by the speed. They stood gripping the pipe of a handrail with one hand, holding automatic rifles with the other, leaning into the wind.

Their pilot sat at the wheel just in front of them; his cap suddenly flew from his almost bald head and stuck, like a scrap of paper on a fan, to the propeller cage.

To the roar of the engine was added the fire-like crackle of reeds and water plants being ripped asunder by the boat that cut through them like a machete.

They approached the peninsula. Ahead was a fragmented view of the church—around which still hung a gray haze of smoke—and the graveyard being reclaimed by the swamp.

Bruno said something.

"What?!" Ferret yelled.

The strong man leaned toward Ferret's ear and shouted, "Local folks say this place is full of ghosts."

Ferret grinned maliciously. "It may be now, thanks to us." He added loudly, "Don't talk, you moron. It was your fault we lost her before—you and your talk!"

"When? When was it my fault? You could have drowned her—remember?"

"Just pay attention to what you're doing!"

Bruno shrugged and returned his attention to the lake ahead. A minute later, he leaned over and said, "Arcane's heat-sensor spotted them from the air, but if it *was* her and the kid, they must have taken one of the smaller channels. They should be on the lake by now.''

"Who else could it have been?" Ferret asked, a shade uncertainly.

"I don't understand this plan anyway," Bruno yelled against the noise of the boat.

Ferret, not taking his eyes from the path ahead, said, "When's the last time you did understand what Arcane was up to? That would be like the mouse understanding the lion."

Bruno pouted. "Well, do you understand him?"

Ferret considered this and gave Bruno a serious answer, although he doubted Bruno would comprehend it. "I understand what he tells me but not what he's dreaming about. It would take a genius like him to do that." He added something he thought Bruno would relate to. "I like the women he brings to the estate, don't you?"

Ferret laughed at Bruno's offended expression.

Bruno squinted and peered ahead. "There she is!" he shouted.

"Pipe down. You want her to hear you?" Ferret said, just to have something to complain about.

It was not until about that time that Cable and Jude heard the sound of the airboat. They were just leaving the mouth of the inlet and heading out into the lake.

The airboat was still some distance away, but the two armed men standing in it were visible plainly enough.

"Government men!" said Jude, alarmed. "I tol' you this place was posted!"

Cable shook her head. "Those aren't government men, Jude."

"Well, thank goodness for that!"

"They're worse."

"Worse than the government? We gotta get outta here!"

He reached to add his muscle to the pole Cable still operated.

Suddenly there was a tremendous animal roar, and in the next instant the huge bulk of something crashed out of the undergrowth at a point halfway between them and the approaching airboat. It dived into the water and disappeared beneath a high-flying splash.

Jude said dryly. "You see that?"

Cable frowned. "Yes."

"Was that a gator—or what?" he quizzed accusingly.

She didn't answer.

Ferret and Bruno saw the thing, too. So did their driver who let the boat drift to a glide.

"You see that?" Ferret asked.

"A moose or something?" Bruno said hopefully.

"Moose! There's no moose around here. It was that thing!"

Bruno nodded. "Where'd it go?"

"I don't know," said Ferret. "But we've got 'em both! Beauty and the—"

The monster popped up twenty feet behind the drifting boat and let out a great screeching howl. Ferret jumped around as if stung by a bee. Bruno spun, let his hand slip off the railing and toppled out of the wildly pitching boat.

Ferret saw the animated green heap only briefly; then it crashed under the water again.

"Ferret!" Bruno screamed, wading shoulder-deep back toward the boat. "Help me! He's gonna get me and pull me under!"

"For Christ's sake," Ferret said, shaking his head admonishingly. "Move, then! Get out of the water!" The cadaverous man aimed his rifle roughly at Bruno. "I'm covering you. If I see him I'll shoot."

"Shoot *him!*" Bruno stressed as he reached the boat and pressed himself up onto its side; the boat lurched and angled with his weight.

Suddenly Ferret caught sight of the monster again. It had surfaced near a jut of land north of them—where another of the natural channels emptied into the lake. Ferret left Bruno to get in by himself and swooped onto the utility box beside the driver. He tore open the roof-shaped lid and grabbed a walkie-talkie.

"Get him!" he yelled into the radio without preliminaries. "He's coming right at you, heading for the channel."

The thing thrashed through the water, heading for the land. He stopped. There was another sound—not just the roar of Ferret's boat revving up again—and it came from the channel. He waded to where he could look down the cavernous leaf-covered channel—the one Cable and Jude had traveled through on their way to the camp—and saw another airboat bank into view. Its flat hull sent a sheet of water off to the side as it turned. This was a newer, sleeker boat than the one on the lake. Three men stood in it; the foremost hunched over a huge 30-caliber machine gun mounted on the prow.

Another airboat just like it careened into view. It, too, had a machine gun.

The creature looked behind him. Ferret's boat was making a wide turn, abandoning its attack on Cable for the moment and acting as backup for the armed fiberglass monsters thundering out of the channel. He was trapped.

He looked again at the two coming at him down the channel. Gunners were ramming ammo belts into their weapons. He submerged and swam back toward Ferret, to deeper waters.

Under water, the creature could hear the boats. He heard the vibrations of the propellers falling in pitch as the boats slowed, waiting for their target to surface.

The water was a bright thick green. Sunlight probed it in wavering shafts that were filled with algae, dirt and motes of decay. Visibility extended only a few feet.

The monster surfaced, breeched like a whale, and tried to take in the positions of his adversaries before he sank again. His enormous lungs expanded with air—but in the oxygen-rich atmosphere of the swamp, there was not sufficient carbon dioxide to sustain his needs for long. He suspected that if he had to, he might stay submerged almost indefinitely, but his instincts told him that he would have to be perfectly inactive for his body to accommodate such an experiment. If he lay still and hid from them, they would get Cable.

There was an island out in the lake . . . maybe if he could reach it . . . but where was it? He was turned around, blind in the thick jade water. He pulled himself along the shallow bottom tugging on water plants, trying not to disturb the surface and reveal his whereabouts.

The water seemed to be getting clearer, shallower. Soon he would be out whether he wanted to be or not.

He had not approached the island—though it was not far—but was on a minor upcropping of land. It supported vegetation despite the fact that its surface remained inches under water. The creature scrambled up onto it, breathing in fierce roaring breaths.

One of the boats strained its engine, the deafening sound a rising jet-like whine, and slashed by the swamp thing in a dive-bomber's scream with a rattling of its machine gun.

The monster howled in rage and pain as the searing bullets slammed through his body, knocking him backwards into the foliage.

He got to his feet, roaring back at the roaring boats.

Ferret's airboat—Ferret and Bruno holding on for dear life—came out of nowhere and struck the submerged land mass. As the airboat sideswiped the creature and sent it tumbling, the slimy land served as a ramp that sent the plane-like boat into the air.

Bruno screamed.

Ferret's boat smashed back into the water; its pilot managed to keep it on an even keel as he shifted gears and made as swift a turn as possible, returning for the kill.

Ferret and his pilot laughed heartily, like rowdies on a fox hunt. But as they returned to the sunken hummock, the creature was gone.

One of the other boats pulled alongside Ferret's slowing vessel. "Did we kill it?" asked the commando at the machine gun.

Ferret shook his head. "Better not have."

Bruno said pathetically, superstitiously, "We'll never kill it. It can't die."

The swamp was eerily quiet with the three airboat engines idling. The third was drifting toward the large island in the lake; the hummock where the creature had been was between it and the other boats.

The swamp creatures were still, frightened. Birds had long since fled the loud scene of battle.

"Damn thing is sure slippery," the commando said to Ferret. "What the hell is it, anyway?"

"That's what Arcane wants to know. We have to catch it to find out."

A large bubble burst on the water's surface. The machine-gunner swiftly aimed at it and fired a short round. Nothing emerged. There were no more bubbles.

Bruno said, "Maybe we better go back for the girl."

Ferret and Bruno twisted around to look back at the inlet where the snail-slow boat had last been seen. It wasn't there.

"Goddamn it," Ferret muttered. He turned to the commando in the faster boat. "Maybe you'd better break off and go pick up—"

Suddenly the boat dipped backwards as the heavy propeller cage was pulled down. The boat turned completely over and both Ferret and Bruno pitched headlong into the swampy lake.

A few seconds later, the creature breeched an incredible distance away and lumbered his way onto the main island.

Bruno and the pilot righted the odd-shaped boat with difficulty. Ferret did not offer to help. He stood in the shallow pea soup staring after the beast, fuming, raging with frustration. He yelled to the other boat: "Go get that frog-faced bastard! Stop him!"

The sleek airboat's props whipped the air as its engine made that rising-turbine noise, and it streaked off toward the island.

The creature was already on the opposite side of the land mass, which was deceptively narrow. It was shaped like a boomerang.

He burst through the low, thick palmettos into view of

the third boat—which was there waiting for him.

The boat's engine roared; the creature roared back at it, tauntingly.

As the boat turned to position itself for firing, the quarry ran along the water's edge, angling around the boat along the bent-crescent shape of the island.

The fusillade began. One shell struck the creature's arm, but he ignored the pain and the flying green matter of his flesh and swerved into the underbrush. Swiftly, out of sight, he made his way down the center of the narrow island and broke into the light on the opposite side. The other powerful boat was there waiting; it revved its engine and followed the creature.

Ferret and Bruno waited and watched from their command ship. They saw the huge mossy brute running in and out of sight, leading a pursuit boat toward the tip of the island. The boat glided a little beyond the tip and then turned, waiting.

The other boat careened around the opposite tip of the island, but because of the bend in the land mass it was not in sight of its companion.

"That's dumb," said Bruno, "the thing's bound to be on the other side by now. Why are both boats on this side?"

Suddenly, the creature burst from the underbrush and headed out into the lake—exactly at the apex of the island. Each boat could see the creature, but not the other boat.

Ferret's hair stood on end as he realized what was about to happen. "No!" he screamed; but his voice was drowned out by the rising roars of the two boats. He grabbed for the walkie-talkie, pressed its button and yelled, "Watch out!"

But his warning was too vague and too late.

The boats plunged ahead gathering speed like dive-bombing banshees. The creature vanished under water and the boats collided head-on at a combined speed of well over a hundred miles an hour!

The crash sounded like a train wreck as the powerful engines and prop cages met in mid-air and the gas tanks exploded. Bodies flew into the air like human cannon-balls, and twisted metal and splintered fiberglass rained into the lake and onto the island. One of the propellers, still spinning at terrific speed, buzzed high into the air and sailed like a Frisbee toward Ferret's boat.

He did not flinch as it whizzed past and splashed into the water.

Bruno stared at the wreckage in horror.

"My God," Ferret gasped, "what *is* that thing?"

The lake was on fire where spilled fuel burned. A man struggled in the blaze, screaming, swimming jerkily. Other men swam or waded toward the island. Two face-down bodies were about to sink.

The swamp thing left the water, unnoticed, and walked back onto the peninsula. His breath came out as hot exhausted steam in the humid, cool morning air. The sun was still low.

The sounds of the swamp began again, timidly.

The creature sank to his knees and lay, grimacing over his myriad wounds, in a soft bed of yielding star moss.

Cable and Jude had found another inlet to hide in. It was a cul-de-sac—they would have to retreat the way they came—but for the time being it seemed to provide safety.

They could not see the battle, but they heard it—the racing boat engines, explosive splashes, terrifying outbursts of machine-gun fire. The great crash that ended in absolute quiet sent them a glimmer of an image in the form of a cloud of fire that shimmered through the trees and reflected from the calm water.

Jude said, "Sounds like World War Three just started."

"Maybe it just ended," Cable said softly, her ears alert.

They heard indistinct shouts, and the sound of a boat engine starting again. It purred this time, at slow speed. The sound seemed to be coming nearer. Cable poled the boat deeper into the underbrush.

From their hiding place, they saw Ferret's airboat. It was almost submerged with the weight of too many men, some of whom were covered with blood.

"One hand grenade would do it," Cable whispered,

observing the single boatload of the retreating army.

Jude said, "You that mad? Killin' mad?"

She thought it over. Her answer surprised her. "As a matter of fact, I am. Mad enough to *plan* killing them." She shook her head in amazement. "That's something I never expected to understand—how that happens in a person's mind."

"That's really somethin'," Jude said with dead seriousness and no trace of condemnation.

Cable looked down at the notebook that rested on top of Jude's old wooden tool box. She looked at Jude, frowning.

"What you up to?" he asked expressionlessly.

She said slowly, "I have to leave you, Jude."

"What you mean?"

"I—I've got to go back and try to help."

"Help? Help who?"

The sound of Ferret's departing boat was now almost impossible to separate from the faint sounds of the swamp.

Cable said tenderly, "I'm not sure."

Jude was completely perplexed. He was about to challenge her.

"Jude, I've got to go," she insisted. "And you have to get his book to safety. Hide it well, and I'll come back for it."

Jude looked at her as if he thought she was crazy. "What's in here?" he asked, taking the book.

She said, "It's what those men are after."

"In one little book? What can—?"

"I'm not sure why they want it so desperately, but I know it's very valuable, to the right people."

"Seems like it's more valuable to the wrong people."

"I mean, to people who would know how to make it work." Her shoulders dropped. "I don't know what else to tell you, Jude. It's complicated and, well, classified."

"Hey lady," Jude said brightly, "you a government man?"

She grinned. "In a way."

He scratched his head trying to integrate this unsavory

142

bit of new information. When he spoke, he seemed to have forgotten it. "Cable, you gonna get yourself killed."

"Will you take care of the notebook?"

"Ain't you 'fraid I'll read it?"

She laughed. "No. *I* can't even read it."

He looked right into her eyes. Then he nodded. "Okay."

Cable gave him a big hug and slipped over the side into the water. "Be careful," she warned. "Stay out of sight."

He watched her climb up the bank onto the peninsula before cautiously poling his skiff toward the mouth of the inlet.

19

By the time it came to a stop, Ferret's boat had taken on water that soaked the boots of the seven standing passengers. The pilot kept the prop turning lightly to combat the current of the river as the men climbed out. They rocked the boat in the process.

"Hey! Easy!" the pilot shouted. More water was sloshing in. The top edge of the airboat was almost under water.

But the men were too eager to disembark. The airboat listed and suddenly, tail first, went down like a rock. It left the pilot, Bruno, and one other commando treading water.

Arcane, grinning, looked down at the men from the railing of his rescue vessel, a great black hump in the water, a hovercraft-yacht that was itself treading water, floating with its powerful blowers temporarily stationary under its rippling black skirt.

Once on board, the men stripped out of wet clothes and rummaged through the assorted ill-fitting garments that happened to be on board. Too few towels were passed around and tossed onto the deck in a damp pile.

Arcane seemed amused by the discomfort of his men and only slightly annoyed at their complete failure.

Ferret said to a still-dripping Bruno: "Ask Arcane right now, and he'll tell you a single battle never wins or loses a war."

Arcane heard him and laughed. "True," he said, "but you aren't allowed the luxury of that particular opinion, Ferret. If you accept that lazy rationale we'll lose every battle—and that *will* lose us the war."

144

Ferret smiled, accepting Arcane's implicit designation of him as supreme commander of the estate's armed forces.

"Under way, sir?" asked a sailor in white who had come on deck from the cabin.

"To where?" Arcane asked him. "No, let's just drift a bit while we think. Don't let the current take us far from the peninsula of our ignominious defeat, however; I suspect we'll head back in that direction." Arcane was seated at a glass table. He spooned breakfast yogurt from a silver chalice.

Bruno wandered out into the sun to let his body dry before attempting to cram his huge thighs into the only trousers that looked remotely big enough. "That thing is smart," he told Arcane. His tone of voice was that of a subordinate giving his report.

"Very smart," Arcane agreed.

"Did you see what he did?" Bruno asked.

"No, but I see the results."

Ferret, his clothes no more oversized than usual, pulled up a chair and sat with Arcane. "That thing planned a trap for the pursuit boats. *Planned* it. Made them collide at top speed."

Arcane slurped a dripping spoonful of yogurt. "This thing has considerable native intelligence," he agreed. "It's surprising. He played a chess game with you and won."

Bruno had sat in another chair and had got the pants up over his calves—which was something of an accomplishment. "I don't get it, Mr. Arcane. Why aren't you mad at us?" he asked.

Arcane smiled at him. "What would that accomplish?" he asked. "Besides, Bruno, in a strange way it evens the odds a trifle. A strong adversary is like a beautiful, dangerous woman. I've never been able to resist either."

Bruno stood and pulled up the khaki pants. They made it to the top, but the fit was wrong everywhere—too tight in the thighs and crotch, too loose at the waist. Bruno reached for the shirt and said, "Thank you for the clothes,

145

Mr. Arcane.''

Arcane smiled. ''Tell the captain to draw anchor, Bruno.''

''We going home?'' Bruno asked, relieved.

''We are not,'' said Arcane. He looked out toward the colorful, sun-brightened marshes. ''He has captured our knights, but in the process, he has exposed his queen.''

Bruno scratched his head.

''Tell the captain, Bruno,'' Ferret said gesturing toward the cabin with a slight toss of his head.

As Bruno walked away, there were two popping rips—his thighs had burst through seams of the trouser legs.

Ferret and Arcane laughed. Bruno said back to them, with surprising self-possession: ''Bet you wish you could do that.''

20

The colossal rat that scurried across her path, Cable mused, was probably a possum; she had never seen one before. It startled her but did not frighten her. The snake she saw was too far away to be a danger; besides, she thought, who can't outrun a snake? She saw no alligators as she ran through the mangrove swamps, but she felt that if she had seen one she'd have merely wished it good morning. Something had clicked inside her; she was no longer so afraid of the swamp.

There were much more dangerous things to fear.

When she could see patches of sky, she looked for traces of black smoke from the wreckage of the airboats. But the air had calmed, and the smoke hung in scattered, low-lying clouds—it seemed to be everywhere and nowhere. The rising sun offered less help in orientation; the rays were too vertical. Cable slowed her passage through the palms and palmettos and ferns.

She was confused. She expected to break into a clearing and see the water of the lake. She saw only a wall of vegetation.

She retraced her steps, found another path, and tried it. She laughed nervously at her predicament. How stupid, after all that had happened, for her to wind up lost.

Suddenly there was a splash. It could not have come from far away, but still she could see no water. Another splash sounded. It was as if people were jumping in, or throwing in something heavy. She walked cautiously toward the sound. The direction took her into wide-open sunlight, which she did not like, but she felt she had no choice.

Cable pushed aside a mat of shrubs and vines and saw that she was on a rise; below her, down a shallow embankment, was the water of the lake. She followed the slope down, keeping behind tree trunks as much as possible.

She stopped at the water's edge, confused. Somehow she had managed to travel in a circle. She was not far from the inlet where she had left Jude. And out on the lake was a fat flying-saucer of a vessel—a black hovercraft she had never seen the likes of before. Sleek and stubby at the same time, it had an elaborate, port-holed cabin—roughly rectangular with rounded corners—and a long chromium-railed deck. At the railing stood a tall aristocratic man dressed in black trousers and black sport shirt. He was talking to three other men, who looked like mercenary soldiers.

He gestured out over the swamp and then turned directly toward Cable. She was in deep shadows and hidden from his view, she felt sure. And yet he kept pointing as if he knew exactly where she was.

Cable stayed frozen until the man left the railing. She was then about to move cautiously back up the bank when a movement caught her eye . . . something in the water.

Jude's boat. It was drifting undirected along the shore-line, spinning in slow motion as it nudged tree trunks in the water.

Jude was lying in the bottom of it, blood covering his skull.

Cable nearly cried out. Tears surged into her eyes, and she started wading toward the drifting skiff.

She heard a sound behind her.

Ferret grabbed her with a shriek of pleasure and locked a terrible hold on her neck. His forearm cut off her scream, almost caused her to faint.

Back at the burned church, the swamp thing waded ashore at the bridge once more. He looked around with mounting anxiety. He tried to call out, and only a roar burst forth. He listened. No one. He ran from one part of the ruin to another. No one. He roared again and listened.

This time he heard the gut-low rumble of a big muffled

148

engine. It was coming from the water. He ran toward it.

He saw a dinghy being hoisted onto a large, black hover-craft. The craft was getting up steam, spewing up a cloud of spray from beneath its air-cushion skirt. When the dinghy was secured over the yacht's fantail, the cloud of spray increased, and the phantom black mound eased off through the trees and was lost in the countless channels of the swamp.

The creature looked frantically toward the inlet where he had seen Cable and the black boy hiding, and ran in that direction. Before he reached the place, he saw the boy's old metal boat caught between trees at the bank, waded to the boat and looked in.

The boy was lying in the bottom of the boat; the bilge-water was crimson. With the greatest gentleness he lifted the light body out and carried it through the water to the land. He smoothed a handful of water over the boy's wound to cleanse it.

The beast laid the boy on deep moss and rested his big mitt over the wound. A narrow shaft of sunlight struck the back of the giant hand and warmed it with life.

The beast laid his other hand on the boy's chest. Was there a heartbeat?

Then—perhaps from the touch, perhaps by chance —one of the boy's eyelids fluttered. It opened. The other eye opened. Nothing in the boy's face moved except his eyes—which opened very wide.

He looked into the face of the monster of the swamp and said, "Ohhhh, shit. There goes the neighborhood."

A huge smile of surprise and delight lit the creature's face. It transformed his fierce visage into something sur-prisingly, achingly human.

Jude raised up on his elbows and took in the creature from top to bottom. He said, "You the dude saved us back there?"

The monster smiled and nodded shyly.

Jude looked at big pockmarks and rips, where bullets had hammered into the beast's body, and his eyes grew somber. "Boy, they sure did a number on you," he said.

He pushed himself to a sitting position and then got woozily to his feet.

The monster shrugged off the boy's concern.

Jude straightened his spine and proudly stuck out his hand. The swamp thing stared at the hand for an instant, amazed and very pleased, then engulfed it in his own huge fist. He tenderly shook it.

Jude temporarily lifted his deadpan facade and grinned from ear to ear. "You're a friend of that Cable, right?"

The massive creature nodded.

"Then I got somethin' I think you oughtta have." He bent forward and reached back into the seat of his pants. "She said I should put this in a safe place," Jude said, extracting the fifteenth notebook.

The creature's distorted face could express yet another emotion: a profound and worshipful joy. His mouth parted, his eyes grew moist, and his cheeks tingled with amazement. He knelt to bring himself to the boy's height and reached out for the book.

The notebook was large and flat in the boy's two hands; in the creature's, it vanished in the way a magician palms a card.

"Need anything else, you just sing out," Jude said, patting the monster's wrist.

The swamp thing studied the boy's small metal skiff and gave him a quizzical look.

They made it work. Along the channel that led to the river where the black hovercraft was last seen, Jude braced himself in the prow of the skiff and poled; The monster sat toward the stern like a big dark mountain—the most imposing passenger Jude was ever likely to have. The stern rode very low; the bow was so high out of the water that Jude's pole barely touched bottom.

Jude's voice floated back to his smiling passenger: "Mama always tol' me not to mess in white folk's troubles. But she never said nothin' 'bout stayin' away from *green* folks."

21

"Chopper Two reporting, sir, returning to the estate if there are no further instructions," said the pilot, alone in his droning, thrumming machine.

"That's the ticket," Arcane's voice said in his earphone.

The chopper pilot could see the hovercraft. It looked like a great black horshoe crab in the center of a blue mist on the waterway ahead of him. He could also see, in the clear midday distance, the plantation with its supernumerary turrets and towers and outlying houses; the estate was situated in what looked like a small golf course in the center of a dwarf jungle on an island almost surrounded by a natural moat of mud.

"Success?" the pilot asked. He had not communicated with them since transferring Ferret and Bruno to their airboat.

"We're not returning empty-handed," Arcane said, "but we have only half our cargo. There's more work to be done."

"I see, sir," said the pilot.

"I'm sure you do. We'll have a moderated celebration this evening, those of us returning hemi-victorious, after we've mapped out a continuing strategy. You might inform the ladies when you land. On second thought, I'll call ahead and tell Caramel and Marsha."

"Strategy, sir?" the pilot asked.

Arcane said, "I rather expect our second guest to crash the party."

"I don't see the airboats. Are they staying behind?"

"Quite permanently. Did you see a plume of black petroleum smoke earlier?"

"Yes, I did. Was that—?"

Arcane said, chattily, "The third boat sank out of lone-

151

liness. Be sure the estate is amply stocked with our various fuels, won't you, Chopper Two? We may have to act quickly in the near future.''

"I'll do that, sir," the pilot said, his mind distracted: What in God's name could have destroyed those boats?

"Fine, Chopper Two. Over and out."

The pilot absently switched off the radio. He was becoming anxious. Clearly there was a powerful danger confronting Arcane about which he had not been adequately briefed.

The hovercraft was directly below. The pilot took a last glance at it—saw Ferret talking to someone on the open deck—and flew on ahead.

While Arcane was below in the radio room, Ferret—out in the sunlight—poured himself a congratulatory drink. As he was about to sip from it, he offered it to Cable instead.

She shook her head slowly, contemptuously.

Ferret said, "You would have gotten away today if you hadn't come back and walked right into our hands."

She said, "Thank you. I assumed it had nothing to do with your intelligence."

Ferret smiled crookedly and sipped his bourbon. "What possessed you to do it? I'd genuinely like to know. I suspect you're not susceptible to whims and impulses."

She ignored him. He watched her eyes size him up: his angular, forceful face; the pirate's earring, his symbol of freedom; his fresh uniform—he was glad he had taken the time to change—the razor-sharp machete on his belt. Ferret assumed that what she saw impressed her, but that she would deny it—perhaps even to her overscrupulous self. There was nothing Ferret was obliged to deny; he found her exciting, arousing even now. Like Arcane, Ferret could never resist a beautiful, dangerous woman. He longed to have her under his power, to have her praying for his control over her, begging him.

He took a step closer. "You could do worse than drink with me," he said, his meaning transparent.

"How?" she asked, dully.

His oily smile faltered.

Bruno stepped to the deck bar. "Can I have a cigarette?" he asked Ferret. He had torn the damaged legs off the trousers and wore them as cut-offs.

Ferret fished him one out of a drawer in the bar; he said to Cable: "Bruno allows himself one cigarette a day. Can you imagine such childish self-discipline. He keeps reminding us all that he's in training. For the Idiot's Olympics, we assume."

Bruno smiled faintly at Cable. She remembered him. He was the one who had wanted Linda Holland's locket. There was a surprising innocence in his face—surprising because Cable assumed he had participated in countless violent crimes. Her assumption kept her from smiling back at him.

The big man turned away shyly, as if he understood her reasoning.

"Where's Arcane?" Cable asked.

"Below," said Ferret. "Busy. See there, in two words I have confirmed your suspicion that Arcane is alive and well, that he is in charge of this affair, that this is his boat, that we are going to his estate, and that he is on board. I'll answer another: he wants that notebook."

Cable regarded the ridiculous man in front of her with fear, interest and overwhelming contempt. "Thanks for the information," she said.

"You see how this works, don't you, Cable? We ask questions and we get answers. I asked you indirectly if you knew about the notebook, and you did not ask, 'What notebook, Mr. Ferret?' What do you suppose that tells me?"

"That I know it exists and what's so important about it," Cable said. She was thinking fast. Ferret did not have the notebook; somehow Jude had managed to hide it before they got to him. If they knew where the notebook was, she supposed, she would be dead by now. Fortunately, Cable herself did not know the exact whereabouts of it; that fact might keep her alive for a while, even if she were drugged or tortured. "Any more questions?" she

153

taunted, her spirits a bit higher.

Ferret chuckled unpleasantly. "Now, that encourages me," he said. "I like a dare. You seem convinced that your willpower is a match for my powers of persuasion. A game ploy, Cable. A match. A challenge for me: how to make you tell me where the notebook is while keeping your body intact for other purposes."

She shuddered and looked away from him. One of the crewmen in white had skin as black as Jude's; she watched him pull in and coil a rope dangling from the dinghy hoist. In her mind's eye she saw the boy's limp arms and the blood on his head. She tried to force herself to believe that he was dead, that she could not hope to find him again. But the inner persuasion did not work; she knew she would look for him and that however slim the chance . . . .

Ferret handed her a drink; this time she absent-mindedly took it and sipped from it. She realized suddenly that Ferret might take her action to be acquiescence; then it occurred to her that she truly did not give a damn what the man thought.

"I'm menacing by nature," Ferret said off-handedly. "But surely you grasp the flattery behind it, Cable."

"In a perverted sort of way," she agreed. She noticed for the first time how unguarded she was. Big Bruno was leaning over the railing paying no attention whatever. One commando kept an eye on her, but he looked lazy and bored. The black crewman was preoccupied.

She turned her back on Ferret. This allowed her to lean over the railing and survey possible escape routes.

"I could do so much for you," Ferret said, pushing close.

She saw a narrow channel intersecting the winding river they had been navigating; there was a little boat there, partially visible through the trees. It reminded her of Jude and his pole.

Ferret caressed her arm. "I could take you out of these dreary swamps and make you fabulously wealthy—if you'd tell me where you hid the notebook."

"I like the swamps just fine," said Cable. "It's the slime that's crawled out from under the rocks that turns my stomach."

Ferret said, "Nasty mouth. But a pretty one."

He gripped her shoulders and turned her to face him. His bony arms drew her in and he kissed her hard. She did not resist.

He released her gently, stroked her hair and said softly, "What do you say to that?"

She moved back a step. "Not much," she answered. With a lightning move she kicked out into Ferret's groin. As he doubled over with a horrendous scream of outrage and pain, she rushed him and gave him a hard shove backward. He went cartwheeling over the side.

Before Ferret hit the water, Cable had vaulted over the railing.

Bruno yelled "Hey!" And a sailor shouted for the captain to stop the ship.

Cable splashed in far from the side of the mist-making boat.

The commando was aiming his pistol when Ferret's voice cut through the air from the water a hundred feet back: "No! She's mine!"

Cable swam frantically until her hand hit the muck at the bottom; she scrambled to her feet, in plain sight for a second, and ran for the thick brambles on the bank.

This was a new kind of swamp—almost impassable. A net of thorn vines tangled in the bushes like cobwebs. Her arms quickly scratched and bleeding, she had no choice but to continue plowing through. The vines that were dead and dry rattled so that she could not hear sounds behind her; but she felt certain Ferret was there. She had caught a glimpse of him in the shallows, his machete flashing in the sunlight.

The roots at her feet were so numerous and intertwined that it was like running on a rigid pile of rain-warped lumber. She felt she was climbing horizontally.

She stopped to breathe and to listen. There were clicking sounds coming from everywhere. She looked at her feet. The ground was alive with thousands of tiny blood-red crabs, stampeding over the roots.

A sharper sound above; it was a huge lizard swishing through the low, matted branches. It stopped to look at her.

Another sound, not far behind her; someone was thrashing through the underbrush.

She pushed ahead, looking frantically for a clear path or some obstruction solid enough to hide behind.

There was a path of sorts, more of a stream in which trickled water dyed red by fallen leaves. She wheeled into it and stumbled, her ankle twisted, got to her feet and hobbled on. The stream seemed to reach a dead end; but she found that it turned under an overhang of branches and continued. She looked back as she turned with the stream. She still could not see Ferret, but from the careless noise he made she guessed he was near the start of the red stream.

She ran, looking down at the treacherous ground, straight into the chest of the swamp thing.

She screamed. The huge, gray-green bulk, the awful face, the flowing, golden eyes! Confused and terrified, Cable turned and ran away, unthinking, back toward Ferret.

At a sound from the thing, though, she realized the monster had not come running after her. She stopped at the branches where the stream turned and looked back at him.

He was holding out his hands to her. The gesture seemed to say: I mean no harm.

She was arrested by the sight. Light came from behind him—there had to be a clearing—and his silhouetted form seemed more colossal and omnipotent than ever. Yet it was not power he radiated; it was pleading.

His gash of a mouth opened. A sound came from him. The mouth moved again, in a face intent with effort. The sound came again. Then he said a single word. It was labored and of such resonance it seemed to come from another world:

"Cable."

She was frozen. Goosebumps thrilled over her flesh and she grabbed a branch to steady herself; she felt faint. She stumbled a step backward.

At that instant Ferret burst out of the underbrush into the red stream. He could see Cable ahead; he could not see what stood in her path. The machete raised high, he lunged toward the branches at the curve in the stream.

Cable saw him, and recovered her senses, just as the machete fell. She dodged, and it whizzed past her ear, chopped completely through a branch, and lodged in a large root.

Ferret was so fierce that he was clumsy. He tugged the blade out of the wood and dived toward Cable again.

She ran the only way open to her: toward the monster that blended so with the vegetation around him that the rage-blinded Ferret had not seen him.

When she reached him, the great green thing raised an arm to protect her from Ferret.

Ferret saw the movement and realized what he faced. As much from sheer terror as from intent, he yelled and swung the machete with all his might. The blade caught that massive right arm just below the shoulder and severed it completely.

Cable backed into the clearing. It was small and almost walled in by incredibly dense vegetation. One break in the trees led to the river. She saw the hovercraft there not far away.

The creature roared in immense anger and pain.

Cable backed into a tree and held it for support. She saw the monster reach out a blindingly fast left arm and grasp Ferret's head—his giant green hand covering the scalp, his powerful fingers falling over Ferret's pallid face and ears.

Ferret screamed. The hideous sound was soul-quenching and final.

Cable saw Ferret's headless body plop to the ground as the swamp thing backed toward her. The creature spun and hurled something dark and round toward the edge of the river.

There was a splash as if a cannonball had hit, and then a boil of armored snouts and tails as alligators discovered the unexpected treat.

Cable lost consciousness and slid down the tree to the ground.

Out in the river, Arcane had come to the deck of his hovercraft in time to hear Cable's scream.

"There!" he pointed toward the shoreline thicket a hundred yards upstream. "Tell the captain to reverse the engines," he instructed a sailor.

Bruno was shielding his eyes Indian-fashion and peering into the swamp beyond the bright river water. "I hope he didn't kill her," Bruno said to Arcane.

"I rather hope so, too, Bruno," he said. "Ferret knows better, of course, but there are times, for men like Ferret, when what he knows is simply not accessible to his brain. Let's hope that he merely incapacitates the lady, so we'll have no more worries about escapes."

"He's crazy, isn't he?" Bruno asked.

"Ferret? I expect so," Arcane said indifferently.

The boat—which had been drifting—powered up slightly, its muffled engines rumbling, water hissing up as mist from the air cushion; and it began to float very slowly back upstream.

They heard Ferret's animal growl even above the boat sounds.

Arcane laughed. "Well, he hasn't killed her yet. He's still doing his terrify-them-into-submission routine."

"He'll give her a heart attack."

Arcane called the black sailor over and instructed him: "Get ready to lower the dinghy to pick up Ferret and the girl."

"Yes, sir," the sailor said with a nod.

Ferret hollered again, but this time something sounded not quite right about it.

Almost immediately the air shook with the terrible familiar roar of the monster.

"Jesus," Bruno said, pale, "it's that swamp thing!"

"Look there!" Arcane said, pointing. "Isn't that the

girl?''

In a small clearing, Cable backed into a tree and steadied herself against it.

The monster—still not in sight—emitted a low rumble that was audible over the sounds of the boat and the swamp; it was followed by Ferret's even louder, terrified howl.

Then there was silence.

The girl sank to the ground.

A ball flew out of the thicket and splashed into the water not far from the shore.

Alligators fought over it.

Bruno shouted, ''*Ferret!*?''

There was no answer. Just the sounds of the gators feeding.

''Maybe we should go in and check,'' said Bruno; ''pick up the girl?''

Arcane shook his head. ''We'll go home now.''

Bruno had never seen Arcane so shaken. ''But sir, Ferret might be hurt.''

Arcane signaled to the sailor not to bother lowering the dinghy.

''Do you remember radio dramas, Bruno? No, I suppose not. They were quite wonderful. Just sounds. And in your mind all the pictures formed while you listened. Didn't any pictures form for you just now?''

Bruno shook his head. ''Shouldn't we check on Ferret? If he's hurt he might not make it back.''

''I think,'' Arcane said looking even more pale, ''that our friend Ferret finally . . . lost his head.''

''You think that thing killed him?''

Arcane nodded.

''Shouldn't we go kill that thing?''

''I still want him alive. The girl, too, for that matter.''

''Well—?''

''Tomorrow is another day, Bruno. Besides, I suspect now that we'll need stronger nets. Go tell the captain to take us home.'' He added, ''We'll keep our electronic eyes on the swamp, never fear.''

22

Cable drifted back to consciousness slowly. She was cool and damp. Disoriented, she wondered hazily what might be wrong with her air conditioner, why her bed should be lumpy, what had happened to the sound of traffic in the streets of Washington—a sound that never completely quit. It must have been about time for the alarm to go off. The breeze . . . was a window left open? That odor of flowers . . . where was that coming from? She thought of cherry blossoms around the national monuments, snow melting.

"How much do you know about artificially induced bio-regenerative activity in plants, Cable? How about laboratory techniques for processing data from organic tests by computer?" asked a kindly white-haired man framed by a window overlooking the library of Congress.

"What a layman can know about gene splicing, work with DNA," she replied; "and almost all anybody knows about data processing for scientific installations in general."

"Ever heard of Dr. Alec Holland?" he asked, lighting a cigar.

Cable felt a fly on her nose and blindly shooed it away. She heard another noise that sounded, in her twilight state, like an enormous fly. She imagined that was what it was, and that it was diving toward her.

The fly became an airboat. She stirred; her body jerked with hypothetical fear. The sound dwindled, faded into a distant locust and a bullfrog.

The bed under her, she realized, was a bed of moss—damp moss—and the lumps were in the tree she leaned against. Her eyes drifted open.

It was the most beautiful spot she had ever seen. The cypresses were like those that had lined the channel she had traveled with Jude, only these trees were taller, more majestic. All of their energies had gone into manufacturing leaves for the thick canopy above; there were very few low branches or leaves. She was in a domed cathedral. The air was more fragrant than any she had ever smelled. Gardenias grew wild among the cypresses, and blooming trumpet vines and orchids stretched up the trunks to reach the sun.

Hundreds of silent butterflies visited the millions of blossoms.

Looking up, Cable noticed that the spokes of sunshine came through tiny holes above at quite an angle; it was late.

That was well and good; it was time to sleep. Still dazed, her mind and body fatigued in the extreme, Cable drank in her surroundings and found them comforting. It was beautiful; that was nice.

She let her eyes drift shut again. It felt as if someone caressed her forehead, touched her hair. That was nice, too.

"Hi," she said to a handsome light-haired man in lab coat and sneakers, "lose a contact lens?"

"Funny," he said.

An orchid grew out of his hand; it branched and exploded into flower as roots coiled around his naked arm. Up and up like Jack's beanstalk grew the orchid. It became a tree touching the clouds. Rain dripped from it, and where the drops fell, green shoots pushed up out of the ground and snaked, growing like a time-lapse photo or a cartoon, into the air till they were a grove of saplings taller than Cable.

Alec leaned down from a high branch of the orchid tree and extended his hand: "Come up with me," he said with a beautiful open smile. But his hand was on fire.

Something cracked into her skull and she fell to the floor of the church foyer. She heard shouts. A blaze swept

161

past her; it screamed in horror and pain.

Her eyes popped open again. Her heart was racing. It surprised her that she was in the cathedral of cypresses she had dreamed about, that it was real, that the sun was really going down. A dozen rabbits hopped about on the moss, pulling up tender blades of grass.

The tree she leaned against moved.

But it couldn't have! She sat bolt upright—weak, her head heavy.

Something small darted through the air near her head. She didn't hear it until it was near; then she remembered the giant fly her dream had conjured. It was a humming-bird. It stopped suddenly in midair, like a helicopter, then darted to a huge orchid blossom.

The blossom was moving toward Cable, bringing the irri-descent little bird with it. The orchid was in an Olympian mossy hand.

Cable jumped to her feet. She had been sleeping against the monster's side, in the crook of its elbow! She remem-bered instantly what it had done to Ferret. Not that the man hadn't deserved it—but the violence of the act was appalling, horrible.

Frightened, she backed away and tripped over a root. She fell awkwardly and sat there staring at him. His big amber eyes blinked. He sat cross-legged like one of those enormous Buddhas in Asian jungles—abandoned, over-grown with moss and vines, but infinitely tranquil and patient.

His only movement was to hold out the flower to her.

She stood and leaned over to take it. She said, as if talk-ing to a brilliant ape or a giant two-year-old, "Very kind. Beautiful orchid."

The monster looked back at her with great intensity.

Suddenly Cable remembered that it had spoken, that it had spoken her name!

He was struggling once again to form words. The first attempt was a rumble, an "Uhhhh." Then he said

162

She knelt in front of him, suddenly no longer frightened.

"Family *orchidaceae*," the great beast rumbled, every syllable an effort. It was obvious that he was learning to talk, and that he would succeed once he learned what was physically required of him. "Genus . . . *orchis*," he said. He stopped and smiled, as if proud of himself.

Cable's mouth hung open in amazement and anticipation.

He went on, a little more ably, "Over . . . a hundred species . . . here. I told you."

She was on her knees before him, holding the orchid to her breast with both hands, her eyes searching his face.

His eyes were watching her face as intently. "I told you . . . much beauty in the swamps . . . if only you . . . look."

A dim ray of sunlight touched his face, gave his grim countenance a marvelous glow. Cable searched it for a likeness, but nothing identifying remained. Still—she knew. Her eyes brimmed over with tears, and after a moment of sharing his difficulty with speech, she muttered, "Alec."

The monster stood, huge and naked. Not Alec at all. Cable gasped and sprang back.

But he made no move toward her; if anything, he shrank back to avoid startling her. He stood there, monumental in the late sunlight, and only waited. He did not look at her.

For the first time she noticed his right shoulder, where an arm should have been, where there was now a ragged stump at which hummingbirds were feeding. He waved his hand to scare them away.

Cable stepped toward him. She could hear his breathing; it was resonant, like that of a horse, big and mighty and wondrous. She touched his forearm. It was soft and hard at the same time, like moss on oak. The tendons that outlined and defined the muscles of his hand felt like grapevine. His breathing remained regal and steady.

She forced herself to look at his terrible wound. It was

163

not like torn human flesh, nor was it like the wood of vegetable limbs; it was a blend of the two with the rough shapes of muscle and bone cut through and oozing a golden sap that attracted hummingbirds.

"I'm sorry," said Cable with great compassion, "It must—"

"Hurt?" he said easily.

"Yes. Does it? I mean, do you feel pain the same way?"

He considered her question. "Only when I laugh," he said.

She stared at him a moment. Something valiant and funny danced in his great amber eyes. Her laugh was short and giddy, incredulous.

His shoulders began to shake, and suddenly his form of laughter was born; it came rolling, thundering out of his chest—a deep helpless wave of fear and hurt and rage all transformed into the release of pure hilarity.

It startled Cable, but soon she was caught up in it—the incredible absurdities, the ridiculous hardships that could only be tolerated when they didn't fit in a sane world, the world she thought she knew.

She laughed at everything that came into her mind. Her scraped and scabbed arms. The mud that caked her from head to foot. A man who wanted to rape her having his head fed to alligators. A man she wanted to love transformed into a monster who terrified her. One complex contradiction after another popped into her mind. She held her aching sides and laughed as she had not done in years.

His laughter faded, and hers turned to tears. She walked into him and laid her face against his chest. His great arm came around to hold her and suddenly rending sobs shook her body. The monster bent low and rested his cheek against her hair.

The sunlight shifted and lowered and reddened. Locusts began their twilight song.

Cable said, against his massive chest, "I'm so afraid, Alec. Have I gone crazy? Is this all a nightmare?"

He said slowly, but with ever-greater ease, "That's what

I keep wondering. I'm afraid, too. *Very* afraid."

"Are you afraid you don't know facts from dreams any more?"

"Everything's a . . . dream . . . when you're alone," he said.

She looked up at him and touched his face.

He breathed in sharply at her touch, and unwanted heavy tears bled from his eyes. "I mustn't . . . hold you," he rumbled.

"Yes, you must," she said, tears returning to her own eyes.

They held each other, frozen, in the gathering mists of twilight.

"Alec, how . . . ?" She did not know how to ask it.

"What happened to me?" he guessed. "I'll tell you. Be patient . . . with my slow voice. I'm learning."

They sat facing each other, leaning against tree trunks. Darkness gathered while they talked.

"Arcane said he hadn't killed you," he said, "but I was afraid he had. He was Ritter . . . impersonating Ritter . . . a mask and a voice."

"That explains quite a bit," she said.

"The formula . . . the one that . . . Linda flicked onto the floor, the one we planted the orchid in . . . I tried to get it away from that maniac. I . . . I was going to throw it into the camp and destroy it. After it combined with every living thing out there on the ground, he would never be able to analyze it, to reproduce it.

"They hit me from behind . . . and the formula sloshed all over me, soaked into my clothes. I . . . I think it spread my capillary action through every fiber of my clothing and then began to penetrate my skin, eating, burning its way in. It . . . it works on animal tissue as it does on vegetable. It replaces cells at a phenomenal rate."

"But why the, the manifestations of plant *forms*, the vine-like vessels, the mossy skin? It did not seem to alter the plants in a corresponding fashion."

He smiled and tipped his head slightly to the side. "You think like a scientist, Alice Cable," he said. "The

165

volatile aspect of the substance caused it to mingle with the plant life in the bog where I ended up. I . . . I thought I was just putting out the fire. No . . . no . . . strictly speaking, at that point, I wasn't thinking. Reflex was rushing me toward the water. All I knew was that I was dying.''

''Oh, Alec!'' she whispered, understanding. ''Why didn't you tell me sooner?''

''My memory wasn't there . . . at least, not all of it. When I fully realized what had happened . . . I didn't want you to see me. I didn't want you to know . . . ever. Then . . . then all I wanted was to tell you. I'm still not really sure why. What's the point of it?''

After a long moment, she said, ''I'm glad you did.''

Fireflies flickered at one another, low over the emerald moss, and an owl fluttered to roost on a high limb.

''I'm not so frightened anymore,'' she said.

He reached back to a deep black hole in a tree and took out the notebook. He showed it to her and said, ''The boy's safe.''

He could see her nod in the blue evening light. He heard her sigh of relief. Though the sky was fast darkening, he saw her face in imagination.

''You're beautiful, Cable,'' he said.

''I know,'' she said, turning him away from a tragic subject with a joke.

But the subject was there—the love they could not have.

It was inordinately dark after sundown, until the moon rose and sent dim gray beams in among the cypresses.

When he could see her face again, he saw that she was asleep, stretched out on the soft moss.

In the middle of the night he lifted her exhausted body and laid it beside him.

23

Cable awoke to the smell of magnolias and the sounds of ten thousand diurnal life forms clicking on with the first of the sun's rays.

She rolled away from the sleeping beast, so as not to awaken him, and got to her feet.

Mist floated along the dewy moss in transluscent clouds and stratified in misty layers up to the high canopy of cypress branches. The leaves at the top were incandescent green.

She stretched and yawned—and looked at her disgracefully dirty hands.

There was the sound of a helicopter among the wild things awakening, but it seemed to be many miles away. Cable looked back at the giant form that was difficult to distinguish against the spread of moss; he had not moved.

A vivid sparkle and dancing reflections off treetrunks told her there was water not far away.

She found a cold, clear, spring-fed pool abuzz with dragonflies and butterflies and hummingbirds. Lilies floated on the water, and hyacinths lined the pebbled shore.

She slipped her clothes off and stepped into the icy water.

Alec had not seemed awake, but as she was walking toward the pool, his eyes had opened slowly and he stared after her.

He walked to the edge of the clearing and watched her bathe from a distance. She was humming a song, softly, blending with the other songs of nature. He turned away, unable to endure the loveliness. He returned to his bed of moss, took the notebook from its most recent hiding place, and read pages of it. Linda's notes were still meaningful to him. He read and relived the experiments, the discoveries, his deep friendship with his sister.

Cable found the pool deep enough in places to swim in, and she delighted in the incredibly clean feeling the world underwater gave her. She examined the pebbles on the bottom and the broad-leafed plants that were miraculously algae-free, as clean as she felt. She dragged her clothes in and scrubbed them clean. She washed the mud of a million nightmares out of her hair.

She did not think of Alec. She couldn't. Her mind cringed from his name as a finger does from a hot stove. She thought of very little, for once, and merely experienced sensations. She felt comfortably alone, not lonely.

While she bathed, sunlight arrived at the pool in long oblique blue-white shafts. The creatures of the daytime increased their calling, whistling, bellowing, and croaking.

She thought she heard the helicopter again but wasn't sure. The last of the mist dissipated while she was on shore rubbing her hair to help it dry in the sun. Her clothes were laid out on warm boulders.

Without warning, three men jumped from concealment and tossed bright-yellow nylon ropes around Cable's naked body.

She screamed inarticulately at first, then managed to yell, "Arcane!"

The man stepped out of shadows as if he'd been called. He said to Cable. "The beast knows my name? My, my, how precocious of it. We know the creature is in love with you, Cable. That's not terribly surprising—now that I see more of you. And I expect it to prove very convenient. Love produces such predictable effects."

In the next instant the swamp thing exploded like a bomb from the jungle underbrush. It crashed and splashed through the shadows, emitting a bestial growl.

Arcane whirled toward the charging monster and shouted triumphantly, "Now!"

Perfectly timed and aimed, a huge net was fired from an

explosive canister; it fanned out in the air and fell over the creature. The creature thrashed about, but he only managed to entangle himself more. The one arm sent him off balance sprawling into the shallows.

Another canister exploded, and another net fell. A third followed for good measure.

The two boldest of Arcane's men, carrying ropes, rushed to the tangle of nets and risked the thrashing arm to get closer. They stitched the three nets together and pulled them into a tighter tangle. Soon the captured beast could not move at all.

The men were drenched from the spray of the fight. Arcane looked at his wet black-silk suit with amusement. "Bruno should be around here someplace," he said to Cable with a chuckle. "He's always telling me I dress impractically." He bent down to look at his netted trophy's face. "Hmmm. There *is* intelligence in those eyes. God, what a brute!"

The men were leering at Cable's body, trying to catch her eye.

Arcane asked one of them, "See if you can find a blanket for our guest. She'll catch cold."

He laughed but said, "Yes, sir," and ran back along the bank of a stream fed by the pool.

"'Fraid I can't risk removing the ropes to let you put your wet clothes back on, Cable. I'm sure you understand. On the other hand, if you'd like to lead us to the notebook . . . no, silly of me to suggest it. You seem determined to keep the epistle out of my hands. Or is it out of *anybody's* hands? You haven't gone and destroyed it, have you?"

"If that's what I've done," said Cable, "how can I prove it to you?"

Arcane smiled and thought it over. "Let's hope it doesn't come to that."

The dozen men were standing around waiting for something. The two victims were bagged—the creature in its nets, the girl roped like a calf.

She bent and fell to her knees in front of the tangle of nets. "Alec," she said softly to the creature.

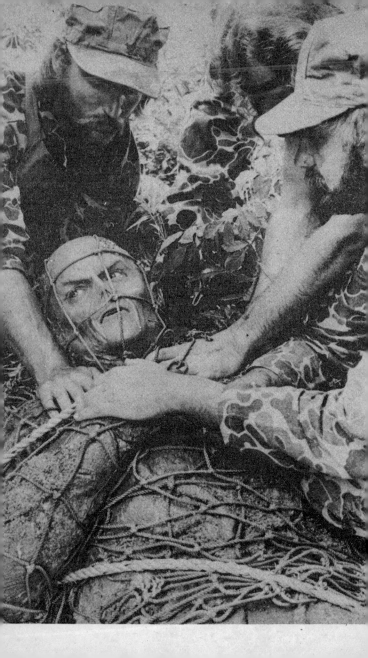

Arcane heard her. "Alec?" he said, "Alec Holland?!" He was thunderstruck. He began to laugh and babble about how he should have guessed.

Cable ignored him. "You knew we'd be caught, didn't you?" she said quietly to Alec.

He said, "The only way out is through."

Bruno walked up at that moment and, with a big smile on his face, placed the fifteenth notebook in Arcane's hands.

"Hah!" said Arcane. "Bruno, you're a genius! Now, remember someone called you that once; it'll do you for a lifetime. Where was it?"

Bruno shrugged. "Lying on the ground."

"Oh," Arcane said, as if the simplicity of the situation canceled his compliment.

"What about the girl?" asked one of the men. "Do we need her now?"

"No, more's the pity, we don't," said Arcane. He added, with a laugh, "John needn't even bring the blanket. Oh, too late; he's here." Arcane himself took the army blanket and draped it around Cable's nude body.

There was a rumble and stutter of a big gas engine coming from the shallow stream. A tall yellow tractor on caterpillar treads bumped and lurched into view.

Bruno asked Arcane quietly, not wanting the other men to hear, "Do you have to kill the girl? I like her."

"Like her? Why, Bruno, you have Thelma, or what'sername, and you have the pick of the flock. What's special about Cable?"

"Don't you think she's special?" Bruno asked. "Not like the others?"

"Indeed," said Arcane. He knew that both Cable and the creature could hear him. "She's especially intelligent, especially informed, especially aware of everything that has transpired here, and outstandingly dangerous. I can't think of a single reason to keep her and ample reason to rid ourselves of her here and now. Before lightning strikes and burns away her ropes, or any such unlikely miracle."

Alec Holland said, "Arcane . . . I'd rather you

171

didn't.'' His voice was paralyzing.

Arcane thought it over while all eyes watched him. "Whatever will make you happy, Alec," he said enigmatically. "Load them both onto the tractor, boys."

24

By noon, Arcane had hurriedly read the fifteenth note-book and had begun to assemble the ingredients needed for the solution. He had feared that something new might be required, something Holland had imported only at the moment of his triumphant success with the mixture; but the final batch was only a rearrangement; not something chemically different from previous samples. Arcane's pantry—patterned as nearly as possible after Holland's—contained everything he needed in order to imagine he was beginning his conquest of the world.

Caramel Kane assisted him. Her luscious blonde hair was tight in a bun; her horn-rimmed glasses hung on a convenient chain around her neck; and she wore a pale green lab smock. She had scrubbed up like a surgeon's assistant and stood at attention letting water drip down her hands and forearms into the elbows of her smock—as she had seen doctors do on television.

"We needn't be quite that sterile," Arcane said, tossing her a towel. "At least," he amended, "I don't think so."

He laid out the chemicals and fired up the burners. Glass heating coils had been blown clean with steam. Spiraling glass condensors sweated a faint vapor from their cooling pipes. A small thermometric titration device was operating, and its buret and stirring motors hummed. A hydrocarbon analyzer buzzed. A still bubbled with water in preparation for the addition of drops of reactant. Pressure was building in the storage tank of the big alkylation device that would combine organic molecules.

"Might as well bring out the cultures, love," he said.

"The animal's labeled *E. coli*; the vegetable's *D complex*."

She tugged open the refrigerator-room door and disappeared for a time into the rows of corpses and parts. "The big containers, Arcane, or the little ones?" she yelled out.

"The little ones," he called back, without taking his eyes from the graduated cylinder he filled with a clear chemical. He dimly heard the klunk of the door closing as Caramel nudged it shut with her bottom.

She stumbled on an oriental carpet in the conversation alcove, and one foot banged down on the floor, but nothing was spilled.

"You must take care, little one," he said, sweating, controlling his temper, when she laid the two containers beside him on the worktable. "You'll find sulfonic acid on the shelf down there—" his head jerked toward the far side of the table "—and a decanter of one-fluro-two-bromobenzene. Bring them. Carefully. Oh, and the benzyl methyl ether."

"Right," she said happily.

Having delivered the chemicals, she stood behind him as he added compounds to a caldron over a blue alcohol flame. Some of them clouded the solution; others cleared it. Some colored; others bleached. Arcane—grumblingly annoyed at the inconvenience of having to do it himself —scribbled notes chronicling the sequence of events. He was marginally cheered by an unbidden thought: someday that very page under his hand might be a museum piece —like the design of the atom bomb that was scribbled on the back of an envelope.

Caramel lost interest in the subtly changing formula and lifted up the tail of Arcane's lab-coat. She slipped one of her cool hands into his midnight-blue linen trousers and let it rest against his gluteus maximus.

When it became clear that he did not even notice, she withdrew and tiptoed to the conversation alcove where she found a technical journal to turn the pages of.

"Caramel—where are you?" he demanded. "Distilled water, quick!"

She watched him add two drops to the yellow substance before him. It kept its hue but turned fluorescent. It looked precisely like the breaker of liquid Arcane had seen in Alec Holland's hand.

Arcane stood down from his stool and took an awed step away from it. "Uh, Caramel," he began hesitantly, "I want you to . . . to contact a few people. Make a note."

She reached for the notebook and ballpoint Arcane had been using. He took the book and tore out the blank back page for her. "Contact Hajj—in Paris, I think, and Dr. Pierre Bouget—who might be in Istanbul."

"How do you spell—?"

He took the page and wrote out the list himself.

"Have Marsha get on the telephone and the short wave and contact these people," he said, handing her the page.

"What is the message?" Caramel asked.

"I expect them here for dinner tonight," said Arcane. "Late dinner to allow them traveling time, say, eleven o'clock. And have the girls prepare the appropriate number of rooms for our guests. Have Marsha tell them I'm taking care of all expenses, and I won't take no for an answer."

"What if they ask what it's all about?"

Arcane estimated his power over them and smiled. "I don't think a single one of them will ask."

While Caramel was delivering the list and instructions, Arcane stared into the beaker of glowing yellow as a wizard peers into a crystal ball. Something—he could only relate it to surface tension—caused the fluid to climb the inside wall of the beaker; and something—the rim of the glass or perhaps the air—kept the liquid inside. He struck it with a stirring rod and the inner light brightened.

Nervously, determined not to spill a drop, he poured a dozen samples into test tubes. He was filling the last when Caramel returned and said loudly:

"Marsha's got on to it already."

Arcane spilled a drop onto the black padded-plastic tabletop. A whoosh of smoke rose from the drop and almost caused him to drop the beaker.

Arcane said to the girl sweetly, "This material is deadly and explosive. If you allow anything at all to startle me, we will probably both die agonizing fiery deaths. Now let's try an experiment with it—or have I frightened you too much?"

"No, I'm not scared," she said.

"I was afraid of that. Go to the greenhouse and get me the smallest samples of, oh, *Dracaena marginata*—they're along the right wall; *Taxodium distichum*, in the back; and a *Helxine solierolii* or two."

"How'm I ever going to—?" she whined.

"They've a skinny cane that looks like a palm tree, a cypress sapling, and some of that baby-tears fern we've got in the kitchen."

Waiting for her, he absently dropped his ballpoint into one of the key test tubes. The plastic softened and melted, combined with the substance, hardened and cracked the test tube. The metal ink-cylinder was unaffected. What he held up looked like some kind of blue popsicle. As he held it, the metal stick got warmer. He could not be sure, but the transluscent blue test-tube-shaped stuff seemed to be getting fatter as he watched it. He poked it with a stirring rod. The material gave; it was not perfectly hard.

While he could still hold the heating stick, he ran with his accident to the door to the outside and flung it out into the tailored yard.

It stuck a magnificent broad live-oak and exploded with a bright blue flash. The tree was engulfed in flame—Arcane could feel the radiant heat—and soon crackled as its own wood caught fire.

The intercom chimed, and Arcane said, before he was asked, "It's all right, I suspect; but have a team make sure that fire doesn't spread. We've just stumbled upon an extraordinary weapon potential, Marsha. One old tree is not too much to sacrifice. Over and out."

Secretly, Arcane breathed a sigh of relief that he had had the notion to throw the thing away rather than put it under a microscope. He made a note of the brand name of the ballpoint while he could still remember it.

Caramel arrived with a tray of small potted plants.

Arcane broke a single leaf from the fern and dropped it in a culture dish that looked empty of formula. He planted a cypress sprout, roots and all, in one of the test tubes; and he dropped another such sprout in another tube sans its roots. The palm-like cane received similar treatment, with various parts of it treated to various concentrations of formula and water.

An hour later, every sample had grown. He took pinches of new leaves and in turn dropped them into other solutions. Shoots grew from them. He took one of the new super leaves and floated it in ordinary distilled water. It, too, sprouted, though more slowly.

After two hours, the work table looked like a potting shed—only there were no pots and no soil.

He trimmed off the taller growths and gave Caramel a handful of greenery. "Take this to the furnace room and burn it up. Quick. And don't drop any of it or take time to talk to anyone along the way."

The cypress sprouts had snapped through their glass containers and sent roots like sluggish earthworms in search of soil. He tried hydrochloric acid on them, half expecting it to fail, but it did kill the rampant growths, shriveling them under a white vapor.

Caramel returned and said, "All done." She tightened the sash of her lab coat and waited for instructions.

"You'll find an arm labeled Darkow in the refrigerator. Bring that out," he said after due deliberation. "It's reasonably fresh."

He cleared a work area in front of him and poured enough formula to just cover the bottom of a culture dish. It glowed when he poured it; its light diminished after it rested a moment.

The arm was intact, neatly disjointed at the shoulder socket. The sample was much too large for the small dish. He positioned the stiff arm so that a gauze pad could be placed over the sliced flesh and bone.

He poured the formula onto the gauze.

Almost at once, the gauze brightened and began to

177

smoke. A yellow life sped through the veins and capillaries of the dead gray arm until the whole arm took on the sunny color. With a mild *foomph* the arm caught fire. Cold flames flickered over it, like alcohol on a Christmas pudding, and then winked out. The yellow arm was left with streaks of black.

The elbow joint softened, and the arm moved slightly. The fingers of the hand curled. Skin began to blister, bubble, and the gas that escaped from the sores smelled of death.

Arcane watched it for thirty minutes, spellbound. The formula had drastically hastened the process of decay. Within a few minutes maggots crawled in and out of the exposed layers, and by the end of his study flies swarmed around it.

Caramel walked over and caught Arcane staring at the putrid arm. "Ugh," she said. But knowing Arcane, she added, "Is this good or bad?"

"Oh," he said with a sigh, "probably neither. I just don't know its principle of behavior. What if the arm had been living, for instance, just cut? No, perhaps that would make no difference. The arm still would not have what it needs—apart from the formula—to support life. An arm is an arm is an arm."

"You're tired," she observed. "Why don't we go get ready for dinner?"

"That's hours yet."

"Uh huh. We can get in that big tub of yours, take a little nap, have a drink or two, and be a bundle of energy when the guests arrive."

He put his arm around her. "You know exactly how to please me."

She chuckled pleasantly. "Sure. You gave me a college course in how to do it."

"You learned well." He turned to face her so she could begin to unbutton his shirt. "I'll bet you've already run our bath water."

"I asked Marsha to do it." She tugged his shirttail out of his trousers.

"Caramel . . . don't you have a thin white gown, something Ophelia-like and innocent and sexy?" He stuck out a shoe for her to untie.

"I guess so; want me to wear it to the party?"

"I want you to lend it to Cable for the evening. You mind?"

She unfastened his belt. "I don't mind." And unzipped him and let the pants fall.

As she led him naked from the room, he said:

"You, Caramel, will be my queen tonight. Wear ermine, and black polyester."

25

All but one of those invited came to dinner; the straggler, it was discovered when the guests compared notes, had died a year earlier.

Ten of the twenty-six were residents or guests of the estate; the outside sixteen flew to small local airstrips in chartered or privately owned aircraft, from the Americas, Africa and Europe. They began to arrive in the early evening in Arcane's limousines and two shuttle copters whose pilots knew how to file misleading flight plans. The guests were accustomed to subterfuge and cunning. As he boarded a copter, the turban-topped Hajj even asked the pilot:

"Are we not to be blindfolded?"

The pilot said graciously, "Arcane only invites those he can risk trusting."

The swarthy North African bobbed his head in approval.

An Oriental from San Francisco disapproved. "Then *I* must risk trusting those whom Arcane risks trusting."

The pilot laughed as he lifted his four passengers into the dark sky. "Arcane respects those who take risks," he said.

The copter banked away from the small landing field, skirted a bayou town, and then left the lights of civilization entirely. The earth was blacker than the cloudy, moonless sky—except for occasional weird smudges of blue phosphorescent marsh gas.

In time, after a flight in a sense-deprivation chamber, they saw Arcane's estate, his little galaxy, as an oasis of electricity in the void.

The helicopter whipped Spanish moss in its storm as it descended past the tops of towering cypresses and landed on the postcard-perfect lawn of the estate near the not-so-perfect black skeleton of the recently incinerated oak. Not a word had been spoken during the trip. As he disembarked, Hajj chuckled, "Blindfolds would have been redundant."

Under the descending whine of helicopter rotors, they heard the nighttime baying of alligators and the evocative screams of ghost birds. And then there was the sound of the second copter approaching.

Marsha and two of the commandos led the guests to their rooms. In the mansion's great echoing foyer, Marsha told them: "Cocktails at ten, dinner at eleven."

There was a shattering crash from somewhere in the house.

Marsha continued unflappably: "Make yourselves at home. There's a game room with billiards and pinballs on this floor. We'll have cocktails in the atrium, and dinner . . . you'll have no trouble finding the dining room."

The crash had come from the lab. One of the plants had not been completely destroyed by acid. A tree had grown out of a wastebasket and knocked over a glass cabinet. Arcane had the tree cut into pieces and burned.

Arcane did not appear at cocktail time, but instead chose to greet each guest as he or she filed in for dinner. He wore a black suede tuxedo, and exquisite bespectacled Caramel, in a stretchy black gown with ermine collar, stood with him.

They were seated around an immense antique table that was inlaid with tortoiseshell and covered by a clear-plastic tablecloth—on which were place settings in a mixture of modern and traditional silver, china and crystal. The chandelier over all was large enough for a theater lobby—of brass, crystal and parchment shades over small electric bulbs.

Arcane was the last to sit. He addressed his guests from the head of the table (Bruno was at the foot).

"I trust you have all met over cocktails; if not, you can attend to omissions later. *I* know you all, and I know how you can be helpful to me in an endeavor I believe will quite literally alter the living habits of each individual on this planet."

Every eye was glued to him as lovely waitresses distributed Wedgewood bowls of cold cucumber soup, and an ancient wine steward set out wine goblets. As if presenting party favors luau-fashion, one of the waitresses presented each of the ladies present with a gardenia.

"You all know I have been at work with the megapotentials of recombinant DNA—the creation of artificial life forms—and that I have placed particular emphasis on the work of Dr. Alec Holland." He leaned forward. "Holland has succeeded beyond my wildest expectations. And I have his formula. *He doesn't.*" Arcane saw that the implications of that were dawning on twenty-five faces.

A commando—dressed in dark suit and tie for the occasion—entered the dining room and leaned to whisper to Arcane.

"Fine," said Arcane. "Bring her in."

Cable, scrubbed and with only a few bruises and scratches showing, looked extraordinarily out of place among the revelers. Her face was not in their world; it was in a world of pain and loneliness and fear. The gown Caramel had lent her was of several layers of a fine white silk. She was barefoot. One of the men—a Britisher named Bailey—got to his feet, moved by her vulnerable beauty.

Two formally dressed commandos led Cable — who seemed either drugged or profoundly weary—to a tall metal and leather desk chair that was an alien among the Louis XV chairs around the table. She was set apart from the table, apparently not to eat.

Arcane cleared his throat and reclaimed his audience's attention. "We have several reasons to celebrate this night. Not the least of which is that we have captured a dragon and rescued a damsel in distress. That's the damsel you see before you, not the dragon."

Bruno, key gunmen, and their ladies laughed and applauded. The foreign guests looked at their host patiently, awaiting more of an explanation.

The commandos clamped irons around Cable's ankles and the legs of her chair. The chair was clumsily bolted to the floor.

The waitress handed a flower to Cable and asked, "Would you like a gardenia?" in precisely the uncaring voice of a stewardess offering cocktails.

Cable took the flower and looked at the girl as if she had to be an escaped lunatic.

Arcane said, "Ladies, take a moment to enjoy your gardenias. Smell them; pin them onto your dresses; slip them into your man's buttonhole." His eyes met Cable's.

If looks could kill, hers would have destroyed Arcane in that instant; but looks are powerless when aimed at an indifferent face. Arcane smiled at her and shook his head.

He stood and signaled to the wine steward to begin pouring. "My friends, my unpleasant duty is to propose the first toast to one who will never join our gatherings again. I think you all knew Ferret."

There were a number of murmurs and surprised looks at Arcane's use of the past tense.

"His frayed and volatile temper has finally destroyed him. He died in heroic and stupid combat earlier today. But he was a valuable cog in the wheel that finally turned Holland's notes over to me. We all regret his loss. Regret it deeply." He smiled a funeral-parlor smile and lifted his glass. "To Ferret."

The assembly echoed his sentiment. "To Ferret!"

Suddenly one of the women jumped and pushed back from the table. "Oh!" she said, alarmed. She acted as if a spider or a mouse were crawling on her. "Get it off!" she said, trying to stay calm. She pulled at the gardenia she had pinned to her blouse.

Arcane stepped over to her. "Don't get excited," he advised sternly. He removed her pin. The gardenia stayed in place. Tiny roots had filtered through the fabric and were growing inside against the woman's breast. He easily pulled the flower off and laid it on the table by her plate.

"Just a root," he said.

She laughed, embarrassed at her foolishness, and took her seat again.

Arcane walked around the table as he talked. "Our real guest of honor tonight is Bruno!" he said with a flourish. He stopped and leaned against the portable mirror-and-marble bar. But for the fact that the muscles around his eyes seemed dead, Arcane was a handsome and powerful figure—proud, straight-laced and casual at the same time, exuding intellectuality. He had just enough gray in his hair to suggest wisdom. "Bruno is our man of the hour."

He took a bottle from the steward's hand and filled his own goblet. As an afterthought, he filled another and walked to Bruno's end of the table carrying both. "If it were not for Bruno, there would be nothing to celebrate. He and he alone found the final Holland notebook, the Rosetta stone that unlocked the future."

The steward bent over Bruno and poured his goblet full.

"To Bruno!" said Arcane.

"To Bruno!" they agreed.

When they had drunk, Arcane handed his extra goblet to Cable, whose chair was near Bruno's. He said to her, rather privately, "I could not imagine you toasting Bruno; instead, you'd have thrown it in his face. But wouldn't you like this, now?"

"Yes," she said numbly. She took it, trying not to touch his flesh.

Hajj said, "Arcane, you are a generous man, we know; but as always with you, the *real* guest of honor at an Arcane gathering is Arcane. What toasts are you reserving for yourself?"

"Yes," another man agreed; "have you tested this formula, created it for yourself?"

Arcane left the bar and strolled back to his seat thoughtfully. "There's no reason to keep anything from any of you—except the formula itself, of course. I have a remarkable and strange tale to tell. I'll tell it while we dine. And meanwhile, you keep an eye on your gardenias."

"Ah!" said a dark woman with a thick accent. "You

treat these gardenia!'' She raised her fork. The flower and stem had sent out tiny tendrils that had fastened themselves around the tines.

The guests laughed and applauded. They immediately checked the gardenias nearest them.

''Each flower,'' said Arcane, ''was sprayed with a solution of one part formula to ten-thousand parts water—which, offhand, seems to be a manageable measure.''

Between salad and the main course (catfish with Creole sauce and truffles) Arcane told the story of Alec Holland's development of the formula, his accident with it, and his transformation.

Cable tried not to listen. His perspective on the tragedy was obscene, and his plan for the use of the formula was the greatest crime she could imagine.

She sipped red wine from the Deco goblet Arcane had given her and thought instead about the past three days. Somehow it was easy, now, to separate the good from the bad—the time with Jude, and the cathedral of cypresses with Alec, and not the pain and the horror. A recurring memory flitted through the rest like a katydid among real leaves: the feel of his skin. Moss on oak. Gentleness and strength. Perhaps, she thought suddenly, the greatest tragedy of all is that Alec has had to become a killer to survive.

She felt fairly certain that he was alive and somewhere on Arcane's property, but she had not been told where.

''How about you, Bruno? More wine, guest of honor?'' Arcane's tone of voice was so different it caught Cable's attention.

''No, I'm fine,'' Bruno said.

The woman sitting at Bruno's right, a brunette with sad eyes and not much of a smile, leaned to Cable and said softly, ''Listen, do you want some food? I think I can get you some.''

Cable took the kindness as genuine and replied, ''No—really. I'm just not hungry.''

The woman nodded.

''The really interesting experiment, it seems to me,''

said Hajj, including the whole table in his statement, "is that which might be done with animal subjects."

A woman shrieked and lifted her gardenia suddenly. "Look! There are two buds—and look at the stem, the new leaves!"

Her specimen was passed from hand to hand while Hajj continued his line of reasoning: "And the ultimate animal test, of course, will be with man."

Several objected—they felt that such experimentation was beside the point. The point, of course, was world domination by means of control of the food supply.

Arcane laughed. "We control the eaten; why not control the eaters as well?"

Hajj stopped the laughter with an angry "No! I have not made myself clear. Under your words, Arcane, under your . . . your almost religious admiration of this swamp thing, there is a suggestion of . . . of . . ."

Arcane supplied it for him in a whisper: "Immortality."

Utensils and wineglasses around the table stopped in mid air.

Arcane said, "Self-sustaining and self-renewing cells. Gentlemen and ladies, I have heard the swamp thing talk! It *is* Alec Holland."

Hajj nodded and asked, his dark bushy brows low over his eyes, "When, Arcane? When do we see the result of human experiment?"

"Tonight," Arcane said casually. "Immediately."

Cable looked at her almost empty wine goblet. A wave of fear shot through her, but she quickly mastered it and said to Arcane: "Have *you* taken it, then?"

He looked at her with magnanimous patience. "No, my dear. I have given the priviledge of taking the first dose to our guest of honor."

Out of a long silence, Bruno said, "Me? Oh, sir, I'd rather not. You know how I hate shots."

There were audible smirks among others of Arcane's men.

Arcane said, "No shots, Bruno. This is something that can be taken orally, or, evidently, even through the pores of the epidermis."

"I don't want to," Bruno said childishly. There were tears in his eyes.

"I'm afraid you already have," Arcane said. "But you can tell it, can't you? You know what I've said is true."

"I don't feel good," Bruno said.

"I expected a quicker reaction," Arcane confessed to the guests. "Perhaps I slipped too moderate a dose into his wine."

As if on cue, the old wine steward brought a corked bottle and set it for safe keeping at Arcane's place.

"Look at *my* gardenia!" said the Britisher, who had stuck one in his buttonhole. It had grown a stem that emerged from the bottom of his lapel with dozens of new leaves and buds. "How long will this grow, do you think?" he asked Arcane.

"Not indefinitely without soil," Arcane said. "It will extend to the limits of the nutrients available within it and then stop—unless it is planted again. It will eventually die —according to Holland's notes—if left alone. But it needs only a small fraction of the nitrogen and minerals and water other plants need. You see, the complete efficiency of the exchange of oxygen and carbon di—"

Bruno screamed. When he did, his jawbone lengthened and his upper teeth pushed forward.

"Oh, my God!" said the Britisher, jumping to his feet.

The woman next to him screamed.

Bruno lashed out in pain and sent china and crystal crashing to the floor.

Cable wanted to look away, but she had to see—no matter how horrible and inhuman this game Arcane was playing. She pulled at the clamps holding her feet to the chair; it was an instinctive reaction to a feeling that what she was about to see would prove so unbearable she must run from the scene.

The massive man tried to stand on his chair. His voice

187

was an endless moan that rose in pitch and volume as if he had no need to breathe. He put a knee on against the table.

His hands gripped the sides of his head and he seemed to be squeezing it into a new shape—long, snoutlike, his eyes narrowing and his forehead shrinking. He clawed at the top of his head as if his skin were burning. Suddenly, a blue flame flickered from his head, down his arm, and winked out at his elbow. He screamed—a high-pitched, childlike sound. Hair fell from his scalp, burning.

The guests had scraped their chairs back and away from Bruno's end of the table.

"Terry!" Bruno rasped.

The woman sitting by Cable jumped to her feet, horrified, and started to go to him.

"Don't," Cable said to her; "you can't help."

Bruno was shrinking. His back was becoming hunched as his spine obeyed the new genetic dictates of his changing body.

He pitched forward onto the table.

Guests scrambled to their feet and backed away.

"Now don't be alarmed," Arcane admonished his guests. "Remember, this is not happening to you! I'm sure this condition will be only temporary. Don't panic." The guests paid no attention. One by one they rose and bolted from the room.

Bruno reached up for the chandelier. Before, he could have reached it while standing on the floor; now he had trouble from the table. He gripped two of the brass bars of it and held on—rattling the myriad crystals—as if hoping to keep himself tall by stretching his body.

His feet left the table. He dangled, whining, crying, as his swaying feet knocked over glasses and bottles, and things crashed to the floor.

Everyone was gone but Cable, Arcane and Bruno.

"I don't understand," muttered Arcane. "I don't understand," he repeated, turning to Cable for an explanation.

She shook her head.

Bruno was a bald midget, his clothes falling off like a circus clown's—with the head of an albino rat.

"Oh, come down from there," Arcane ordered, annoyed.

Bruno obeyed. He dropped onto the table and sat in the middle of the mess crying like a baby. "What did you do?" he whimpered.

"What did *you* do is more the question," Arcane said. "Look what you've done to this place."

Bruno picked up someone's fork and played in someone's plate of fish much as a child with a shovel plays in a sand box. "I should've died," he said softly.

Arcane sighed and said, "It's always darkest before the dawn. Let's pay a visit to the genius who really authored tonight's disaster."

26

Arcane's mansion was antebellum; part of its understructure dated from even earlier times, when the area had been a lawless frontier.

The procession that descended to the catacombs beneath the laboratory was a queer one. Arcane had pried open his tight collar for comfort but otherwise looked formally dressed; Bruno—a hunched, snouted dwarf—had been re-dressed in rags that more nearly fit him; Cable was barefoot and frail in her flimsy diaphanous gown that did nothing to ward off the chill of the cellars. Behind them trotted two armed guards in tuxedos; and in the rear two lab technicians in smocks struggled with a handtruck of heavy equipment and a fat electrical cord which unrolled from a spool on wheels that bounced along the irregular paving stones of the floor.

Mice squealed and darted into holes and darker corners. One of the guards who had a penchant for neatness burned out spiderwebs as his blazing torch passed near them.

They passed a zoo of sorts. In small rooms with jail doors and high slits of windows cowered whining wolves with dogs' heads, diseased deer, a wildcat with no hind legs and several domestic dogs with various malformations. The creatures whined and growled as flickering torchlight disturbed them and passed them by.

In the last cage before a spiral descent, two men in khaki rags clutched their bars, watching the procession go by. "For God's sake, Arcane," said one of them in a trembling voice, "enough is enough."

The lab technician reeling out the power cord stopped at

the cage and whispered, "Damn, Henderson, I thought you were dead!"

The grimy bearded man shook his head in the dwindling torchlight. "He put us here six months ago. He thought we were cowards 'cause we told him we were going squirrelly at that swamp camp."

The technician commented callously as he hurried to catch up with his mates: "You're lucky."

The spiraling stone stairs, supported by rotting beams thick as tree trunks, led to a large room crisscrossed with beams like the underside of an old railroad trestle. This room, too, had a row of window slits at the high ceiling; but no light streamed in from the black night—only a damp mist rolled in from the marshes.

The swamp thing, difficult to pick out at first in the wavering light, was chained to a huge X of timbers, which in turn was chained to the trestle posts of the aged dungeon.

They kept Cable and the others on a landing, hidden from sight, while Arcane alone approached the creature that had been Alec Holland.

"Your formula is more complex than we thought," Arcane said, thinly disguising the turmoil behind his casual words.

A low rumbling chuckle came from the chest of the thing. "Ah, it's *my* formula again. I had not even begun to test it. I have no idea how 'complex' it is. What have you done with Cable?"

Arcane studied the creature; in the light of his torch, it looked weak, sagging on its chains—pale, if such a thing is possible for a tree. But it was still monumental, with a look of superhuman strength. And the eyes danced.

"You *are* in there, aren't you, Holland? All of you. Your brain is intact. You have everything you had — and now physical power besides, and . . . and everlasting life."

Holland said, "You could kill me in a minute, Arcane."

Arcane sloughed off the fine point. "Barring accidents,

of course. You can live as long as you want to here, Alec.''

"As long as I help you."

"Of course. That's the agreement we reached this morning in the swamp, isn't it?"

"It wasn't my life I was bargaining for at the time."

"But the effect is rather similar."

"Where is Cable?"

"Not far away and in good health, I promise you. I'd like you to earn an opportunity to see her." He yelled toward the eroded circular stairs: "Bring Bruno!" An afterthought: "And the equipment."

Alec did not laugh when he saw the bald human rodent that still had some of Bruno's qualities: the face still looked oddly innocent in combination with its furtive cowering shape; his stubby arms and legs retained their muscular definition, though all hint of stature had been lost. The sight was not amusing; it was pathetic.

"You gave him the formula?" Alec surmised.

"And he shriveled up into this! Why?" Arcane stood with fists on his hips expecting an answer.

"I—I'm not sure," said Holland within the beast.

"But you think you know. You *will* tell me." He motioned for the two technicians to lower the monster to the ground.

The technician who had spoken to the caged men said, "It'll take more than two of us to do that." He gestured, indicating the size and shape of the beast and the timbers.

"Don't you know about pulleys and leverage?" Arcane asked sarcastically. "I'll help you. The top chains lead to a winch. Crank that down gradually and pull his feet out at the bottom. Plug up and let's get some light in here!"

A harsh floodlight illuminated the sagging green monster as they began to tip him and crank him down.

Alec's eyes met Bruno's.

The rodent man said, "Does it hurt where your arm is gone?"

Alec smiled; he remembered the answer he had given Cable. "Not much anymore," he said.

"That's significant," muttered Arcane as he puttered

with the equipment on the hand truck.

Bruno asked the giant, "I won't change back, will I?"

Alec had always hated the hollow and helpless feeling of pity. "I don't think so," he said honestly. "The . . . your new cells are so much stronger than the old ones, they will resist any attempt at alteration."

"Am I going to live forever . . . like *this*?" the dwarf asked, horrified.

Alec turned away and could not answer.

They had lowered Alec in steps; now the last turn of the winch set him on the ground.

Alec laughed as they approached with electrodes and Arcane set dials on a glowing box. "Are you planning to torture me?" he asked. "To force me to do what? Tell you what?"

"My dear Dr. Holland, what do you take me for? You're not to be tortured. You're about to receive your first physical as a thing of the swamp rather than a man. I have to know what's inside you."

"Why not dissect me and see directly?"

Arcane smiled crookedly, "Oh, I should hate to do that." As he attached electrodes from the cardiograph, he mused, "Do you suppose you could survive dissection, doctor? Could I remove your head and, say, plant it in my kitchen window box—so you'd be there when I needed to consult you, be there powerless to move or even to do yourself harm? Would that work, do you suppose?"

"Try it," the creature suggested.

"Ah," said Arcane. "You don't think it would work. Sad that you currently place so little importance on your own survival." He clicked switches on and off several times. "Machine's on the fritz. Wouldn't you know?"

"I don't think so," said a technician. "I think he has no heartbeat. There is activity, though," he said, pointing to an unsteady line at the bottom of the graph.

"A sort of vibration," Arcane said in wonderment.

"No blood pressure," said the other technician who had just checked for it in the creature's one arm.

In spite of himself, Alec said, "That's interesting. I can

193

feel a slow heartbeat."

"We'll see about that," said Arcane. He asked the technicians: "Set up the portable fluoroscope." He mumbled, removing the electrodes, "We'd need to inject a dye to do this properly; oh well, we'll see what can be seen."

While setting the scope in place, Arcane philosophized, "Odd, Alec. I envied you your genius when I kept an eye on you as Ritter. It was not your lab I wanted to possess, it was your mind. Now that's changed. I'll settle for my own brain, thank you, but I'd change bodies with you in a second."

"Now that you've robbed my brain of what you wanted from it," Alec surmised.

Arcane chuckled inanely, happily. "Say 'Ahhh,'" he said switching on the scope.

Alec read amazement on Arcane's face and asked, "What do you see?"

Arcane shook his head as he fumbled for words. "The shapes are there, but not as sharply defined. Everything —skin, bones, organs, fluids—is of roughly the same density. Vegetable! The heart . . . it's there but smaller, working very slowly, incredibly slowly, to move the . . . the *sap* through your veins!

"There's a bullet lodged in your left ventricle—in the very muscle of it—and it seems to have no effect whatever! Other bullets that would be fatal to a human are lodged in your lungs and other organs. You are truly a marvel! And to think you're bored with life!"

After using a crude chromatograph, Arcane had a result on the gas exchange in that creature nature had never intended:

"What you exhale has almost the composition of what you inhale. You extract a trifle more nitrogen and carbon dioxide and exhale less than the equivalent in oxygen. How do you account, incidentally, for your essentially vegetable nature and Bruno's conspicuous lack of chlorophyll?"

Alec answered with a bored sigh, "I was under water, surrounded by plant life when I was transformed. It combined with my molecules. And . . . ." Alec trailed off; a thought had suddenly come to him.

"Go on," Arcane insisted.

Alec smiled. "I have an affinity for plants. Always have had."

Arcane thought for a moment, tilted his head, and peered into the creature's fantastic expressionless face. It was lighted harshly by the one floodlight that had been clipped to a huge nail.

"Are you suggesting," Arcane asked, "that there is a psychological determinant in the transformation?"

"Ask Bruno," Alec advised.

"Bruno can't tell me the time if he's wearing two watches," said Arcane.

Bruno walked—waddled like a short-legged duck—to look down into the monster's face. "What do you mean?"

Alec looked up from the X of timbers to which he was chained. Of the two, the standing midget looked more helpless and susceptible to hurt. Because Bruno had guessed it.

Arcane said, "I want to know what we did wrong, Holland. We followed your notebooks religiously. There is precious little margin for error."

"There was no error," Alec said, his voice rumbling majestically from his chest. He was still looking up at Bruno—who suddenly hid his face in his hands.

Arcane pressed: "I want to know why Bruno there does not have your strength."

"Because he never had it," Alec said quietly.

Arcane got to his feet and motioned for the technicians to pack up the gear. He said angrily to his adversary, "No riddles, please. You'll tell me or pay a heavy price. Your own life has no value for you, but we have the trump card you yourself suggested we hold over you." He yelled toward the stairs. "Bring her down!"

Bruno turned and wandered into the dark slashes of shadows. His beady eyes were dry and staring.

They held Cable at the foot of the stairs and Arcane pivoted the floodlight to single her out. "What is it to be,

Dr. Holland? The corrected formula—or Cable? Which?''

Alec had never seen her look so lovely. Her brown hair had been washed and dressed; she wore a little makeup and the white dress accentuated the litheness and fortitude of her body. Her bare feet made of her a supernatural spirit of woodlands.

"Don't help him, Alec," Cable pleaded.

He said to her helplessly, a world of wistfulness and longing in his voice, "I *can't* help him."

The statement was so forlorn that Arcane had no choice but to believe it. "Why can't you?" he asked simply.

"You don't understand," Holland said to the ersatz scientist who bent over him, "there's nothing wrong. Nothing hidden. No secret for me to tell you. The formula works in such a simple and direct way. What Bruno took was precisely the same as what changed me. It . . . it amplifies your essence—not just your physical characteristics. It takes the deepest, strongest urges of the soul as a directive factor, a code for reassembly. It simply makes you more of what you already are."

Arcane had picked up the torch and was lighting it again with a cigarette lighter. "You're saying that since Bruno's essence was stupidity, the formula has simply extended, amplified this trait to ridiculous forms and proportions?"

Alec said, "I doubt if it involves his native intelligence. Rather—"

Arcane ignored him and continued his own line of thought: "But if the essence of the subject is genius, this genius shall be made monumental in body as well as intellect. You're right, Alec. It's beautifully simple."

At Arcane's signal, the floodlight was turned off and the others preceded him up the steps. As he reached the stone stairs, Arcane looked at Cable, then turned to Alec and said jauntily, "I'll take it myself."

He turned and disappeared into the stairwell. His flickering torch bounced light back at changing angles as he climbed. It stopped when there was only a faint reflection left, and there was the clanging sound of a door of metal bars being jammed into place. Then the light and the bumping thumping sounds faded completely.

It was pitch dark.

Cable fumbled her way to Alec's sprawled, chained body. She sat on the timbers next to him.

"Cable," he said simply.

"Alec," she said in reply.

And volumes of feeling passed between them.

They heard something bump in the blackness among the timbers. "It's just me," Bruno informed them.

Cable leaned close and ran her hand across Alec's massive brow. Somehow his skin seemed softer, less resistant. It felt cold.

"Do you have any matches, Bruno?" Cable asked.

"No," he said. "Sorry." He had blundered his way through the cross-braces and was close by.

"Tell me what did it," Bruno asked Alec.

Alec did not answer. In the dark, his hand had found Cable's and he felt the touch of her fingers on his massive palm.

"Please," Bruno asked again.

"I think," Alec said, his voice rumbling in the rock and timber chamber, "you kept yourself small, Bruno, and made yourself stupid. So that you would not have to make changes you saw were necessary, you pretended not to see. Pretty soon you weren't pretending any more. You had made yourself conveniently blind."

"I—I wanted to be a big man," Bruno whispered.

Alec said kindly but without mercy, "You made yourself a big something, but from what you've become now, I don't think you were much of a man."

"No," Bruno agreed. "If I get better, can I change back?"

Alec said, reflecting talks he had had with himself, "You have to live with yourself whatever form you find yourself in. You can't ever count on going back."

Cable lay on the damp rocky floor and used Alec's chained hand as a pillow. "We have to stop Arcane," she said.

He said nothing. After a moment he began to laugh.

"What's the matter?" Bruno asked sharply, alarmed at the sound.

"He's laughing," Cable said, puzzled.

Alec said, "A long time ago I saw this cartoon. Two men in rags were chained, hands and feet, to an immense stone wall. There was no floor down as far as you could see, and the ceiling, half a mile up, had a tiny grate in it. The situation was preposterously hopeless. And one of the ragged, bearded men turns to the other and says, "Now here's my plan.""

Cable snorted. "Oh," she said.

Alec laughed again, and Cable joined him. She stopped and wiped her eyes and said, "What do you know—I'm not going to cry this time."

"I didn't think you would," he said.

27

Unshaven, his jacket discarded, Arcane stood at one of the narrow Tudor windows of his laboratory and looked out toward the swamps. Dawn was some time away, but the sky had lightened to charcoal. He could make out lake-like layers of fog out of which towered ink-black silhouettes of moss-covered cypresses and live oaks. He brushed a fly from his ear.

The laboratory was teeming. In the humid air, a mere vapor from Holland's substance had accelerated and exaggerated the growth of insects—which reproduced at a prodigious rate—and plants.

Earlier Arcane had leaned exhausted over his worktable and dozed—and dreamed of all the things in his refrigerator coming to life and parading out after him.

He walked through a cloud of gnats on his way from the window, and at the table he once again sloshed acid on new soilless sprouts of fern *prothallia* that had burst from spores settling out of the air—some of them green and growing even before alighting. In the conversation alcove, fern *prothallia* had mated to form new ferns, whose roots searched the upholstery, carpet fibers and woodwork for nutrients.

Mysterious vines grew up the legs of his work stool, and moss colored the walls in growing patches.

The air smelled rich with ozone, as after a spring rain.

These matters struck Arcane as mere nuisances to be overlooked for the moment. He had before him a beaker of the solution, a trifle stronger than that which Bruno had drunk; and deadly immortality beckoned to him through its pale amber color.

Did he hesitate? He would have said no. He would have said the scientist in him urged caution while the romantic grasped at the dare.

The notebook beside him was filled with his own notes: his sketch of the incident with Bruno, his findings upon examining the swamp thing—which he did not call Alec Holland, in preparation for claiming Holland's discoveries as his own—and his declaration of intent to experiment with his own body for the advancement of science. The exact concentration of the solution in the beaker before him had been noted with great precision. In contrast to Linda Holland's shorthand scribbling, Arcane's penmanship had artistic flourish and was difficult to read only where he was uncertain of his data.

The lab was dim, dungeonesque except for the pools of light made by the high spots; and the buzz of flies and gnats was joined by something larger that sounded like a wasp but had not shown itself. He pulled a sprout from the floorboards and laid it across his work table out of idle curiosity: would it continue to grow?

How long before the vapor in the air would have an effect on Arcane himself? He estimated it to be a matter of weeks, unless the vapor concentration changed.

His eye roved from the beaker of full-strength solution to his diluted mixture intended for consumption. The mixture seemed richer than it had. Arcane wondered suddenly if, due to the reproduction of microorganisms within it, it grew stronger by the minute. And what of the full-strength solution: *was* it full strength, or was it increasing also?

He took a wine glass and poured his mixture into it. It brightened like yellow phosphorus and then began to dim. He carried the glass with him to the intercom panel and pressed a call button.

By the time there was an answering knock at the door, Arcane had returned to the window to look out at the ever-lightening sky.

"Hi," said a lovely woman at the door, rubbing her eyes. "What can I do for you?"

"Come here," he requested. "I'm distracted. I've forgotten your name."

"Nola," she said kittenishly, stepping full into a

spotlight. She had long blonde hair, an exquisite mouth, an unbelievable shape, and she wore glasses. She had been a guest of a guest at dinner; and due to a most generous offer had elected to join the estate. "This your lab? It's kinky. I like it."

"Would you bring me a brandy, please, Nola?"

"Sure. Be right back." She made a gliding turn that flounced her transparent night shift.

When she was gone he looked back at the swamp. Over the jungle of gray shapes there was a pink opalescence in the clearing sky.

He toasted the dawn with the living concoction in his wine glass, and tossed it down in a single swallow.

In the colonial catacombs beneath him, others watched the high windows burn pink. They had talked very little in the past hours—just enough to know that no one slept.

Suddenly a cloud slipped by, and a ray of sunlight broke into the dungeon. It struck high on the heavy timbers opposite the window.

Alec said weakly, "Cable!"

"Yes Alec?" she said, concerned.

"The sun . . . I must reach the sun. I have no strength."

She looked at him in the gloomy light. His eyes were barely open, and he seemed unable even to lift his hand. Tears came to her eyes and she angrily wiped them away. "Is there a way we can reflect it?" she asked.

"I don't know," Alec murmured; the words were barely discernible from the rasp that rumbled from his chest.

"If I . . . if I climb up there, Alec, is my white dress enough to—?"

"No. Too indirect. Can you work the winch?"

"Oh! Of course," she said. "Will that raise you high enough?"

"Almost. I think."

The chains rattled through pulleys until they were taut, until the hard part began. Pushing with all her might, Cable was able to cause only one click of the ratchet. But it lifted the timbers Alec was attached to an eighth of an inch off the ground.

Bruno took the crank away from Cable. He said, "I got to have a few muscles left, lady. Let me try."

The ratchet clicked, clicked again, clicked again and again. The X of wood lifted slowly off the floor.

Alec's head was in the angle of the shape; it fell through, bent back, bobbed like an unconscious man's head as the timbers slowly, one jolt at a time, raised him like a ship's anchor.

The chain around his waist dug into him, and the chain at his wrist felt as though it would pull off his remaining arm. He groaned in pain.

"Stop!" Cable told Bruno.

But Alec managed to whisper; "No—go ahead. Quickly!"

The ratchet continued to click. Bruno had to hook his shriveled bare feet under the iron stanchions of the winch to maintain his leverage and purchase. With each turn of the crank he emitted a garbled grunt of effort. His turns began to slow.

"I'll help you," Cable said, adding her weight to each downward thrust of the crank.

Soon the X of timbers was upright, back where it had been before.

He was still a foot or two short of reaching the sun's rays.

Hard as they tried, Cable and Bruno could not budge the crank with the full weight of his five hundred pounds plus the weight of the wood. He could not be lifted any higher.

Cable ran around to him. With his waist tied at the axis of the X, his feet were off the ground, sagging in tangles of chain. His head leaned against his arm.

"You have to do the rest, Alec," she challenged him. He did not stir.

She pounded on his leg. "Wake up, damn you!"

"I'm awake, Cable," he said slowly. "But it's no use."

"The hell it is! Look, you can reach it if you try. It's not far!"

He looked down at her and smiled. His eyes opened a

little wider.

"Look up there, not at me. Reach for it, Alec!"

He raised his limp hand and aimed it above him. It almost touched the ray in which peach-colored dust particles boiled.

"Higher, Alec. You can do it! Please. Do it for me. For all of us," she pleaded.

She suddenly rushed to his feet. "Bruno! Help me get a loop of chain under each foot. He can push up on them!"

Alec said, straining, almost inaudibly, "Just under the left foot."

They managed. The chains rattled and creaked as he pushed upward. His finger tips reached into the ray. They seemed to glow with the brightness. Almost at once his body trembled, and with a little more strength he pulled up higher, until his open palm was a shining god's hand of green brass.

In Arcane's laboratory, the same pink rays cut through the small square panes and lighted the busy air inside.

Arcane held a clock in his hands resentfully, as if calling it a liar. So much time could not have passed.

There was a knock at the door.

"Come in," he barked.

Nola backed in with a breakfast tray—covered dishes, orange juice, toast, and a large snifter of brandy.

"I just wanted brandy," he said, his anger diffusing with the sight of her. She had taken time, while the tray was being prepared, to make herself look spectacularly alluring.

"You always keep flies in your lab?" she asked as she set the tray on the table in front of him. "Gee, you need a shave."

"Do you care?" he asked, amused. His anxiety over the clock was almost a thing of the past. "Come here."

Her raised eyebrows said: Oh, we shouldn't—not on an empty stomach. But she obediently drifted into his arms and kissed him. "I like a man to have a beard," she warbled.

He took the brandy and handed her the orange juice.

"Apparently," he said, "I *am* what I've always looked like."

"Huh?"

"Nothing. You were there last night. How long did it take for Bruno to . . . what's wrong?"

She was staring at his face, frowning. "Your beard," she said tentatively, "it's longer—"

"Longer than what?"

She dropped the orange juice.

"What's the matter with you?"

She couldn't speak. She pointed at his hand, or was it the glass of brandy?

He looked closely. The back of his hand was bubbling, breaking; but a brown foam, not blood, oozed out of it.

"Go—go—leave me!" Arcane insisted.

She was riveted to the spot, horror-stricken. Her eyes moved to his arms.

The skin was softening, as a hard dry sponge softens with water; the skin began to flow, sag, run, and that brown foam boiled up from the many tiny rips.

Arcane dropped the brandy and cried out in pain.

Nola screamed and ran from the room, leaving the door standing open after her. Arcane took a step to follow and then stopped, paralyzed. His entire body seemed to be on fire. His clothes began to smolder.

Nola's screaming wakened the house. There were shouts and footsteps.

One of the gunmen ran in his underwear. "What's wr—?" And stopped dead in his tracks. "Jesus!"

Arcane's back was to him and as the back grew in breadth, the fabric of his shirt pulled apart in a zigzag rip. The skin that pushed through was brown and boiling.

Arcane staggered to a wall mirror and looked at himself. The face that looked back at him was moving, widening, lengthening. His eyes were red, bulging, blowing up like tiny balloons. He screamed and looked away. He was dimly aware of a clot of people by the door, staring at him; his image of them was red and wavering. He staggered to the work bench to hold himself erect against it.

He missed the edge he grabbed for because as he lunged his frame shot up a good ten inches. He fell against the lab stool and sent it clattering to the floor. He fell to his knees. His vision grew darker, more blurred, and soon he could see nothing before him.

His comrades and servants watched in abject terror. They saw his clothes rip away as his body swelled. His rib cage became enormous, and as it expanded the brown viscous substance bubbled out from between the ribs and covered the skin of his torso and trunk.

Skin literally fell from his legs—to be replaced by the fast-expanding foam and something that looked like scales.

The foam began to harden; it piled around him, covered him from head to foot. It hardened and cracked and was replaced by more foam from inside.

It hardened into a carapace of ugly umber crust. Arcane was inside it, not moving.

His followers stared at the titanic cocoon; a few of them took steps closer.

Suddenly the crust was broken by the emergence of something white and bony and hard; another followed beside it. They looked like tusks. The whole brown shape quivered. Some of the surface broke off and shattered to dust.

Then something scratched from inside, like a great bird attempting to hatch itself. A chunk of the brown substance fell away as something like a set of talons pushed out. The talons clawed back, breaking off more of the shell. Another hand—if that was what it was—broke through and ripped more of the shell away.

A terrible deep snarling wail boomed from the monstrous egg as it shattered from within and what was Arcane rose to its full height. He was a horrendous hyena-faced monster—lion-maned and covered with clumps of gray hair—seven or eight feet tall and apparently still growing. His teeth had turned to savage tusks, two of which protruded like those of a wild boar, and his hands were the huge scrawny reptilian claws that had ripped from the shell.

The monster saw itself in the wall mirror and recoiled, backing against the worktable. A massive mutant arm slashed out and demolished the glass condensers over the table.

The house staff had backed out the door, and most had fled. A few stood riveted with fascination. Even they turned and ran when the monstrosity let out a terrifying screech that carried to every corner of the estate.

Still he grew. His legs developed enormous thighs and spindly sinewy calves. He toppled off balance and crashed into the worktable. The formula spilled and flowed across the black tabletop and splashed onto the floor.

A billow of blinding, yellow fire erupted from the floorboards and engulfed the worktable.

The thing reached into the fire to rescue his notebook, but withdrew his burning hand screaming in pain.

A flash of yellow flame flickered over him like St. Elmo's fire, consumed him briefly and then winked out.

Then he listened. His supersensitive ears had heard a sound, a sound even his agonized brain could easily identify. It came from below, in the dungeons.

Arcane coughed out a shrill, deafening explosion of fury and staggered—gaining confidence with each step—to a display of ancient armaments decorating a far wall. He clawed at the brackets and flung aside shields and pikes to reach an enormous sword.

The laboratory in flames, Arcane—now a giant of muscle and armor-plated scales, a nightmarish amalgam of bestiality, still growing—charged toward the door leading to the dungeons below. Mindless of barricades that stop ordinary men, he crashed through the door—tearing through the lumber of the frame and several feet into the wall on top and sides of the opening.

He announced his coming with another shriek to wake the dead.

Behind him, his staff had begun to salvage whatever was portable of their private possessions; there was no fire department near enough to call.

28

As Nola was delivering Arcane's brandy and breakfast tray, Alec Holland's green hand was pushing up into the solitary ray of sunlight brightening the dungeon below.

The angle of light was such that as the sun rose the ray quickly expanded, reached deeper and deeper into the big wet room of rock and timbers. As it descended, more of the flesh of the swamp thing fell under its beneficent warmth.

With his returning strength, Alec stretched up higher, breathed deeper, exercised his muscles.

His feet pushed down under the chains, and thin tendrils grew out from his toes toward the rocks of the floor. He lifted his head higher into the sunlight.

"Alec!" Cable shouted suddenly. "Your arm!"

On his right side, where his arm had been, something waved up. A vine-like tube of wiry green flesh and sinew, split at the end into coiling tentacles, grew out of his shoulder.

The roots from his feet touched the floor and made their way between the ancient stones into the rich black earth below.

"Godamighty, I wonder if I can do that," Bruno muttered, staring up at the magnificent moss-encrusted giant that was becoming whole again.

The network of roots that wrapped Alec's body began to move, travel, grow. New shoots reached down from his shoulder for the forming arm and entwined it.

Alec held the new hand in front of his face; already the fingers had shape, and he had control over them. He lifted his new flesh into the sunlight. He raised his arms and flexed revitalized muscles of iron throughout his body.

The chains at his wrist and waist and legs screamed at the strain and gave way.

Pieces of chain and padlocks clanged and gonged against the rock wall and the leaning timbers. The sound echoed loudly up the rock staircase and into the corridors of the house, and the laboratory above.

Alec slipped from the hanging X of timbers and severed the root tendrils that had temporarily linked him to the earth. "Let's go!" he rumbled. He led them to the circular stone staircase that rose to the corridors and the mansion.

Halfway up, Cable stopped him and said, "Listen!"

It came again: an awesome roaring shriek that rolled like a hurricane down to the cellars.

Alec said, petrified, "He's taken the formula!"

They reached the top of the stairs and faced a grate of heavy iron bars. Alec tugged at them, to no avail. He braced himself and attempted to pull the entire grate out from its slot in solid rock. The rock chipped and splintered; but the grate would not move easily or quickly.

The beast that was Arcane howled again, from much closer, and now they could hear his lumbering footsteps.

Alec tugged harder at the grate. Smoke began to filter down the corridor toward them.

One of the two men in the cell down the rock corridor yelled, "Holy shit! The place is on fire! Hey, somebody, let us out!"

"We'll be burned alive!" yelled the other.

The far end of the corridor was lighted by a fixture over the stairs leading down to it. Alec and Cable and Bruno saw that light dim, saw an enormous shadow falling in its place.

Then they saw him. He stepped into view with smoke snaking around him; he scarcely fit into the shape of the tunnel.

He had to dip to keep from bumping his boar-like head, and he lumbered from side to side smashing into the animal cages, freeing the wretched creatures by accident. The deformities danced around his gigantic canine legs. Sparks flashed where his blade struck rock and metal.

Alec had still not managed to loosen the grate; and now he was not so sure that that would be desirable.

One of the imprisoned men screamed with terror as the apparition crashed into his cage; but the collision wedged open the bars enough to release the men.

Bruno banged on Alec's arm. "Stop! Stop! I know a way!"

The little rodent man led them back down the stone stairs. "If you can't get out that way," he said to Alec, "he can't get in that way."

Alec said soberly, "He's a lot bigger than I am, and a lot madder."

As if he heard—and perhaps he did—the Arcane monstrosity shrieked his cry that was neither animal nor human, but the most alarming aspects of both.

Back in their dungeon, Cable stumbled as they hurried to the far end of it. "Ignore me!" she insisted. "I'm barefoot, and I just stepped on a sharp rock; that's all."

Bruno pointed to a torch bracket high on the wall. "If you can reach that," he said to Alec, "turn it."

When Alec pulled on the bracket, there was a rumbling sound of counterweights falling, and a metal door that was set under the foundation timbers cranked open.

Alec and Cable looked at Bruno in amazement.

The little creature said, "They put it there in case a guard ever got shut in by mistake, I guess."

Before the three could exit by the newfound door they heard the grate at the top of the stairs: it bent with a screech and the rock around it shattered loose and rattled down the stairs.

In a windowless passageway, Cable looked back briefly toward the metal door.

"I don't know how to close it," Bruno said.

Alec gave it one try—it bent but didn't budge—and they left it open.

The tunnel led down. There was a hint of light from ahead; they hurried toward it. Bruno rode on Alec's enormous shoulder like a mouse-navigator, pointing out the path at intersections with other dark tunnels.

The deafening howl of Arcane echoed around them; he had entered the tunnels through the metal door and was not far behind them.

They broke into a circular room with a vent at the top through which a little light seeped. In the center of the rock floor was a black pool of water approximately eight feet in diameter.

Another roar came from even closer. Arcane had not made the mistake of wasting time searching side corridors. He was right behind them.

The room was a dead end. There were no doors, no windows, only a small opening out of reach twenty feet above.

"He's trapped us!" Cable said. "The little bastard can't resist helping his old master, even after—"

"No!" said Bruno. "This is your only way out. But . . . but you have to trust me."

"What do you have in mind?" Alec asked.

Bruno said, "This is the well of the estate. It's fed by springs. If you swim out, you'll come up in the swamp. Can you hold your breath?"

Terrified, Cable nodded. "If I can swim fast enough."

"Then go!" said Bruno. "Maybe I can slow him down."

Cable jumped into the icy water with the great green monster of the swamp.

There was another bellow from Arcane.

Bruno—too small to be noticed by the hellish Arcane—ran back along the corridor and threw himself at the beast's spindly feet.

Arcane went sprawling.

Bruno disappeared into the shadowy tunnels with a giggle of triumph.

The swamp thing was a powerful and fast swimmer; he held Cable against him and fought his way up the current of the spring.

There was no light at first, only a direction of flow; finally a glow appeared ahead. At last the light spread around them and they kicked, their lungs about to burst, to the surface.

It was like the pool where Cable had bathed and been caught; only this one was smaller and deeper. Early morning mist obscured the wide roots of cypresses.

They pulled themselves onto the shore and collapsed.

Arcane boiled up from the pool with the force of an underwater explosion.

Now he had reached his full identity: he was truly monstrous. Eight or nine feet in height, he leapt onto the land and shook water off in a huge spray, like a wolf-god. His sword flashed in the bright sunlight, and he emitted his fearsome cry.

Alec backed to his feet and tried to shield Cable behind him.

The towering beast was upon them in a single jump. His ancient sword, gripped as in a vise by his talon-like fingers, sailed elegantly through the air.

"What's there to gain from this?" Alec's voice rumbled from the chest of the swamp thing. "You have what you wanted, Arcane."

But the gruesome tower of scales and hair and talons and fangs merely snarled brainlessly, voicelessly, and circled, looking for a swift kill.

"Now comes the fun part, Arcane," Alec said, always keeping himself between the monster and Cable, "learning to talk. You don't have time for this silly vengeance."
vengeance."

The gleaming medieval sword, an evil Excalibur, fell with incredible speed. Alec lunged to one side, hoping the sword would strike the bolder beneath him: surely no blade could endure such a destructive blow.

But with ever-sharpening reflexes, Arcane stopped the metal millimeters before it met the stone and swerved the blade to follow the dodging giant.

The blade cut through Alec's calf. He shouted and stumbled, but rose swiftly to his feet, wielding a boulder which he hefted into Arcane's scaly gut. The monster stumbled back with a roar of outrage and stumbled into the water.

"Quick!" Alec said to Cable, "get out of here. Run!"

"No," she protested, "I won't leave—"

"I can't concentrate," Alec said, "with you here, and he knows it. He knows my mind is in two places at once; I don't know whether to protect you or attack him. Now go!"

Reluctantly, she backed toward the high trees at the rim of the pool. She was horrified by the thought of being unable to help—though she knew intellectually that such an advent was impossible—and by the thought that she would not know what was happening.

Arcane raged out of the water—his coverings and appendages seemed to lift half the pool out with him—and went straight toward Cable.

Alec threw himself into the air and slammed into the monster's side. He bounced back. Arcane was bigger and heavier and had braced himself for the blow.

A sound like a million snakes came from Arcane's body. It was laughter. He raised the sword to chop at Cable and then altered his direction and lunged for Alec's neck. His obscene laughter grew mightier. Alec ducked.

Too late, Alec realized that Arcane had maneuvered both of them so that they were trapped with their backs to the deep pool. Arcane's sword flashed again.

Arcane was more powerful, but Alec was far more agile. Alec danced away from the blade. Arcane growled, a high-pitched cat-like snarl. He laughed again; evidently his animal impersonations amused him.

Suddenly Alec lost his footing on a mossy rock. He was slightly off-balance, and the blade was coming, stabbing forward.

"Alec, look out!" Cable shouted, trying to shove him out of harm's way. Arcane's sword struck Cable in the chest and penetrated deep. She crumpled and collapsed on the mossy rocks.

29

Arcane, too, seemed startled by the mortal wound he had inflicted. Momentarily, the two great unnatural beasts were still.

The rumble that rose was not distant thunder; it came from the swamp thing. Bottomless anger had been released. As he stood to full height—his arms raised toward the sun, his fists closing—the intellect of Alec Holland stepped aside for an awesome animal rage.

Arcane took a step backward—a grave tactical error that showed he could still experience fear. He seemed to forget for the moment that he held a sword, that he was not the elegantly dressed Arcane plotting strategy but was, rather, the artillery itself.

Alec leapt from a boulder that gave him height almost equal to Arcane's and clutched the thing's broad, hairy neck. The two creatures toppled to the ground. The sword fell from Arcane's talons and splashed into a stagnant stretch of mud.

Arcane tossed Alec away with a thrust of his powerful legs and scrambled to retrieve the sword.

Stinging particles of dirt shot from the sword's edge as Arcane swiped it again and again through the air.

Alec backed away from the pool into thicker underbrush where the sword would be more difficult to use. A wildcat snarled and bit into Alec's leg: Alec had stepped into a nest with cubs. Instinctively, Alec ran at an angle to lead the rampaging monster away from the nest.

An explosion drummed the air; smoke was mixing with the mist of morning. Arcane seemed to hesitate a moment as he registered the meaning of the sound: it was a helicopter taking off.

The hesitation gave Alec an opportunity to grip the beast around the neck and to pull back and back and back. Arcane's deadly fangs bit deep into Alec's forearm. Alec screamed in pain and fell away.

His fangs, his fangs . . . now that Arcane had discovered their use, he lunged, drooling, for Alec's neck as his talons dug into his side and abdomen.

Alec had never felt fear like this; it was immediate and desperate and overwhelming. He fell to his knees and slipped out of the monster's grasp temporarily by somersaulting away between its legs.

Alec's hand grabbed a cypress trunk for support. The tree was dead; it broke and came away in his giant hand. Scarcely thinking, Alec wielded it like a club and smashed it into the side of Arcane's head.

Arcane wavered, stunned.

Alec struck again, and Arcane fell, thundered, to the ground.

Alec looked frantically for the sword but did not see it; it had been knocked away, out of sight.

The beast that was a composite of everything vicious in nature lay in a puddle of slimy mud.

Alec ran back to the pool, to Cable.

He lifted her tenderly into his ripped and shredded arms. Blood ran from the hole in her breast and crimsoned the front of her white dress with a horrible spreading stain. Alec's eyes fogged with amber tears.

"You were right," she said without opening her eyes, "about the swamp. It is . . . beautiful." Her eyes flickered open for a moment, and she lifted a white hand to his cheek.

Then the hand fell.

He gasped, frantic, denying the possibility of losing her. He looked around as if there were someone who might come to help if he called. Then, his face suddenly intent, he reached with his powerful hand and pulled a wad of his own flesh from his side.

Still grimacing from the self-inflicted pain, he laid it,

dripping with its peculiar golden sap, over her naked breast and forced it into her wound.

The pressure of his hand roused her, awakened a last glimmer of consciousness, and she opened her eyes to look at him.

She looked past him.

She managed to whisper, "Alec! Behind you!"

In a motion of incredible swiftness, Alec laid Cable on the ground and rolled out from under Arcane's downward swing. The tip of the blade struck a stone and rang like a bell; its point broke off and spun through the air.

Suddenly determined, fearless at last, invincible, Swamp Thing walked directly toward the beast of Arcane.

Arcane took an involuntary step back. He stood more than two feet taller than Swamp Thing and surpassed him in weaponry; yet he was momentarily frightened. Swamp Thing looked unstoppable. He raised the sword with less certainty and lowered it with less confidence.

Swamp Thing stopped that blade-brandishing, taloned claw in mid-air and wrenched the weapon from it.

With all his might, Swamp Thing swung the blade and caught Arcane just as he was turning to retreat. The blade split him asunder from the neck to the belly.

Great coils of green veining sprang out of the vast wound, and the bubbles of brown foam released a heavy yellow fume when they burst.

The great armored body teetered. Its legs ossified and shriveled. Its eyes exploded. And the carcass fell with a crash into the water of the spring.

The water—which had been crystalline—turned the murky color of quicksand.

Swamp Thing watched the bubbles that were a sign of rapid decay. Arcane had been theatrical to the end—concerned with the appearance of the power and not efficacy itself; obsessed with the appearance of genius, not the dedication and application that supports it; preferring to terrify, rather than to cooperate. Arcane's transformation had suited him exactly.

There were shouts in the distance, and the starting of

automobiles. A voluminous plume of black smoke streaked westward in the morning sky, like the outpouring of a smoldering volcano. A cracking explosion rattled the air and a balloon of boiling fire shot up over the trees.

Swamp Thing bent to Cable's body. As he had done once before, he gently pushed the hair from her face. She did not stir.

He lifted her limp form, cradled it in his arms, and walked with her into the swamp.

The mist was evaporating; the little lives of the daytime were out in force, singing, chirping, croaking.

30

Swamp Thing carried her to the cathedral of cypresses and rested her on a bed of plush moss.

Her heart still beat, tentatively, and now and again she would breathe. The compress of his flesh had quickly stopped the bleeding. But she did not awaken. Her body did not feel feverish; on the contrary, it felt cool: insufficient life coursed through it. He used Arcane's sword to slice loose a blanket of moss, and covered her with it.

He gathered wild fruits and mushrooms for her to eat; but she would not wake up to eat them. A piece of hard cypress root made a convenient bowl; but she would not turn and drink the water from it.

He stood in the vast enclosure of lush blossoms and a circular colonnade of trees. He looked to the sky and to the earth for answers—and received only a tranquil presence for a reply.

Mid-afternoon, Cable stirred and mumbled in her sleep.

He ran to her. She called his name and cried for help— and then turned to lie still again.

Swamp Thing hurried into the swamp. Following streams and subtle landmarks, he located the trapper's cabin. There he found Jude, still in hiding.

"Everything okay now?" he asked the mossy giant that towered over him. He looked at his battered arms and legs and said, "Man, you just can't stay outta trouble."

"Cable's hurt. She's going to need your help."

"How 'bout the bad guys?"

Swamp Thing smiled and reported, "I don't think there are any left."

The deadpan Jude said, "Hate to see 'em if they look wors'n you do." He switched off his portable radio.

"Can you bring a blanket?" Alec asked.

"I got a quilt."

"That's fine."

"Food? Med'cine?" Jude asked, tossing Alec a faded, hand-made quilt. Alec stood in the doorway and effectively blocked most of the afternoon light. "I hafta pole over to the station and get some stuff. Where's she at?"

Swamp Thing gave the boy directions and returned to the clearing at a run.

He found Cable lying very still under the blanket of moss. Her eyes were open, blinking. He lowered himself beside her.

"Hi," he said, his voice resonant, rumbling.

She smiled. "Thanks. For whatever you did."

He peeled away the moss covering and replaced it with Jude's quilt. "This ought to be cleaner, and warmer," he said softly.

She pushed the quilt back with a weak hand and looked at her chest—at the green and yellow compress. She touched it lightly. It felt warm. "I don't understand," she said, frowning. "Arcane—"

Swamp Thing nodded, smiling, his eyes moist. "Arcane with his terrible swift sword. Leave that there a while. It's healing."

"You killed him?" she asked.

"Yes, I certainly did. Chopped him in two." He laughed.

"Is that what's got you in such a good mood?"

He was lying beside her, his head propped by an elbow. A tear ran sideways down his cheek, traveling slowly like molasses, and touched his hand. "No," he said, wiping it away. He noticed that her smiling eyes were studying his face—his hideous overblown burned-out green face—and he sat up to turn away from her.

"What did I say? What's wrong?" she asked.

His mind foraged for alternatives. He would have given his life to find something that would change things, some-

thing he had overlooked in his hours of thinking and dreaming.

"It's over," he said.

By his tone of voice she knew he was not referring to Arcane. "Alec—no. Let me stay with you. We'll find a way to start your work again."

He spun around on his knees and faced her, holding out his giant hands. "With these?" he asked angrily. Then he calmed himself and sat back on his heels. "With these?" he asked again, matter-of-factly.

She raised herself to one elbow. "I'll be your hands."

He smiled sadly and shook his head. His big right hand reached out and touched her hair.

"Alec—please!"

He said, "You need . . . you need to heal. You need to look at the world again."

Tears came to her eyes. "I can't leave you alone."

"I won't be alone," he said. "Not the way I was— never again, thanks to you."

He got to his feet and did not look down at her.

"Alec!" she cried.

"I'll see you again," he said, still riveted to the spot.

Cable felt desperate, but she could not think what to say. In her mind's eye she saw the handsome man in the blue boat who had taken her out to show her his world.

The huge, vine-entangled creature who stood over her, his back to her, ran a hand across his face and then walked quickly away toward the edge of the domed clearing.

She sat up and watched him moving through the shadowy trunks and into the gathering late-afternoon mist.

There was a sound nearby; something was moving in the underbrush. Cable's heart raced; it would take her a long time to rid herself of jumpiness and sudden terrors.

Jude stepped into the clearing. With his tool box in one hand and a blue box of bandages in the other, he looked a little like a small doctor.

Cable smiled at him. "Jude," she said simply.

The boy opened his box and extracted a Coke. He snapped off the cap and handed it to her. "The big guy tol' me to come get you.'' His eyes widened at the sight of blood dried all over her dress. ''You okay?''

Cable's nod was all she could manage for him. She was staring out into the mist.

Alec was part of the life of the wilderness now and almost immune to its dangers. Man was the danger to him, as man was the danger to the swamp. He would study the songs of birds and the cycles of ferns and the habits of dragonflies.

He would learn to read the wind.